★

CHRISTMAS PRESENCE

★

By the time Arabella had stripped down to her bra and pants, she knew for certain she was being watched.

She tossed the bra onto the bed, a casual movement, but her eyes were triangulating every square inch of the room and her mind was working furiously to check and correlate data. Notions of two-way mirrors, eyeholes in paintings, and secret passages behind the wainscotting were considered and discarded.

There was something frightening but at the same time rather exciting in this blind-man's-buff striptease, she thought, as she lay back on the bed and began to ease off her pants.

Then she had it. In the ceiling panels, above the ornate pseudo-candelabra, a knot-hole that wasn't. Nothing so startling as an actual eye peering whitely down at her, in fact no real evidence at all. But she knew . . .

RED CHRISTMAS

Patrick Ruell

MYSTERIOUS PRESS

THE MYSTERIOUS PRESS • New York

For Des and Kathie

MYSTERIOUS PRESS EDITION

Copyright © 1972 by Patrick Ruell
All rights reserved.

This Mysterious Press Edition is published by arrangement with
the author.

Cover design by Rolf Erickson
Cover illustration by Danny Smythe

Mysterious Press books are published in association with
Warner Books, Inc.
666 Fifth Avenue
New York, N.Y. 10103

A Warner Communications Company

Printed in the United States of America

First Mysterious Press Printing: May, 1987

10 9 8 7 6 5 4 3 2 1

How many old recollections . . . does Christmas time awaken!

We write these words now, many miles distant from the spot at which . . . we met on that day, a merry and joyous circle. Many of the hearts that throbbed so gaily then, have ceased to beat; many of the looks that shone so brightly then, have ceased to glow; the hands that we grasped have grown cold; the eyes we sought have hid their lustre in the grave . . .

CHARLES DICKENS *The Pickwick Papers*

1

*This way—this way—capital fun—lots of beer
—hogsheads; rounds of beef—bullocks; mus-
tard—cartloads; glorious day—down with you
—make yourself at home—glad to see you—
very.*

MR. ALFRED JINGLE

There was a movement in the copse and a cock pheasant came
out, fast and low. The taller of the two gamekeepers instinctively tracked it with his gun barrel, an easy, rhythmic movement that advertised a first-rate shot.

His companion, however, kept his eyes fixed intently on the
copse. Only the haze of his breath in the frosty air belied his
complete stillness.

'Fox?' said the taller man. 'Or probably nothing. God,
these leggings are killing me.'

The other relaxed and shrugged.

'Probably. You shouldn't lace them so tight.'

'Wardle likes us to look smart. Here, fancy a drop?'

He produced a gun-metal flask out of the capacious pocket
of his tweed jacket.

'Wardle wouldn't like that either.'

'Then the fat bastard can lump it.'

He took a long draught, replaced the flask and glanced at his watch.

'Nearly twelve. Time to get down to the road and make like the loyal peasantry. Anyone interesting on today's guest-list? Aren't the Froggies coming?'

The other man did not reply, but with one final long look towards the copse, he began to make his way down the frost-sprinkled slope on which they stood towards the line of hawthorn hedge below which marked the road.

Behind him, his gun now broken as a concession to the treacherous surface on which they walked, the tall man followed, still talking.

'Hope there's a pretty face among this lot. Have you seen that German cow? A right case of udder-shudder there. Hang on a sec, I'll have to loosen these leggings. I'm sure that smooth bastard Boswell's got it all wrong. I've never seen anyone on a Christmas card looking like us.'

The smaller man stopped and turned.

'You talk too much,' he said equably.

'I'm sorry if it bothers you.'

'No. It doesn't bother me.'

There was a slight stress on the last word.

In silence, they resumed their progress down the hill.

The man in the copse smiled as he watched them go. He had been smiling as he watched them approach also. There had been a time when the heady pleasure this kind of situation sent bubbling along his bloodstream had caused him some concern. But now he accepted it, even looked forward to it.

In the old canvas bag by his side were two fat rabbits and a pheasant, still warm. Not a bad half-hour's work. It was surprising what enjoyment there was to be got out of this poaching. Swiftly he separated the short barrel of his shotgun from the stock and slid them into the specially prepared pockets in the lining of his old combat-jacket. Below, the two gamekeepers were mere matchstick men against the white of the frosted grass.

The poacher began making his way uphill, keeping the copse between himself and the descending men. He moved with easy efficiency. At the brow of the slope he paused, glancing down again, his keen eye following the line of hawthorn which marked the road. From his pocket he produced a small telescope, a child's toy in appearance. But he was quite happy with its performance. Quickly he focussed on a curve where the hedge was broken and the metalled surface of the road was visible from this elevation.

For a minute or two there was nothing. Then his face broke into the lively attractive smile which it wore so often. Ridiculous, artificial, corny, it might be. But the sight below gladdened his heart.

Into his view trotted four fine bay horses pulling behind them, glorious in reds, yellows and browns, a tall nineteenth-century mail-coach.

As he watched, he saw the guard, in anticipation of their approaching encounter with the gamekeepers, raise his shining key-bugle to his lips and a few seconds later the lively, harbingering notes vibrated to him through the keen, cold air. Then the coach disappeared behind the tall hedgerow once more, its passage marked only by the coachman's cocked hat and the highest peaks of the luggage strapped on to the roof.

A fine, fine sight. Who was in it? he wondered. What strangers with hearts eager for what kind of joys, seasonal or unseasonal, were being carried along to their destination? A romantic thought!

But as long as they were strangers to him he could wish them all well. As indeed he did to all men, even the gamekeepers.

For today was, after all, Christmas Eve.

Unaware of the seasonal greetings that were being offered them from above, the four passengers in the coach were reacting to their journey in different ways.

They had introduced themselves five miles earlier at the railway station (or, more properly, railway halt) when it was established that they were all intending coach passengers. *Intending* was perhaps too strong.

A dark, thin-faced, ascetic-looking man had spoken in rapid French to the vivacious brunette with him when they saw

9

the coach and then asked the coachman in slightly over-perfect English, 'Is it not possible to be driven by taxi?'

'No no, please, Jules!' cried the brunette before the coachman could reply. 'The coach, she is lovely. We must go in her to be *or-then-tique, n'est-ce pas*? It is necessary.'

To Miss Arabella Allen, possessed of all the knowing cynicism of a twenty-three-year-old English virgin, it seemed that Madame Suzie Leclerc's English was slightly over-Frenchified, its quaint charm being aimed at the ear of the fourth passenger, a young man of almost feminine beauty. Arabella felt her own strong jaw-line assume the proportions of a Bob Hope alongside the delicacy of this youth's bone structure.

His name it appeared was Stephen Swinburne and his nervous smile in reply to Suzie's plea for support was taken as positive agreement. This, and the fact that, apart from the rapidly disappearing train, the coach was the only vehicle in sight, finally persuaded Monsieur Leclerc to climb aboard.

The presence inside of a small oil-heater and a lot of travelling rugs cheered him up to some small extent. The coachman and guard fitted the luggage on top and very quickly, with a rousing fanfare from the guard and a cracking of his whip from the driver, they were on their way.

'Have you been to Dingley Dell before?' Arabella asked the beautiful youth.

'No,' he said in a low-pitched upper-class voice. 'The place hasn't been going very long, has it? Anyway, I usually spend Christmas with friends, but this year I was talked into a spot of family togetherness. And this is where Mummy and Daddy decided to come. They've been down since yesterday. I can't say I'd been looking forward to it much. Till now.'

Not so shy, decided Arabella. The man is not the mannerism.

'What about you, Miss . . . Allen, did you say?'

'That's it. No. I had noticed the adverts, *Have Yourself A Dickensian Christmas*, and when my other plans fell through at the last minute, I decided to book here.'

'You were lucky. I believe they get very fully booked very quickly.'

10

Arabella shrugged.

'Perhaps there's not much call for singles. At Christmas.'

Suzie decided that it was time she made her presence felt in the conversation, though the expensive aroma which emanated from her ensured she would not be ignored.

'We come for a real English Christmas, you understand? Jules, he works in London for many years. But every Christmas, home we fly to Paris for two, three, days. Then back again. This year I say, Jules let us for once spend Christmas over there, in England. No, better, let us pass it in the old-fashioned England, like on the Christmas cards. Some of my friends they tell me of this place, Dell. So here we are!'

'*Dingley* Dell,' said her husband.

'That's what I say. Dinkley Dell. Like in your Dickens' *Pickwick Papers*. I have read. See!'

Triumphantly she produced a paperback edition of *The Pickwick Papers* out of the large and very expensive-looking fur muff she wore.

If the book-match folder sticking out of the volume marked her place, she hadn't got very far, thought Arabella.

She turned her attention to the countryside they were passing through. They had very rapidly turned off the secondary road which passed by the railway halt on to an even narrower road, scarcely more than a lane, though the surface was metalled. The landscape, made breathtakingly beautful (in every sense) by the gleaming sprinkling of frost, was pleasantly varied without being dramatic.

Small hills, woods, folds of land, ploughed fields like frozen seascapes, some sheep, cows, a black horse running down to the hedge to greet its passing fellows, the occasional sheepfold or distant farmhouse—there was very little here to disturb the illusion that this journey was indeed being made in the first half of the nineteenth century. And at Dingley Dell itself, so the brochure had assured her, even the telephone wires had (at huge expense) been laid underground for greater verisimilitude.

It would probably be vile. All kinds of pseudo-jollities. Still, whatever it was like, it would be a change from last Christmas with the temperature at eighty degrees in the shade. A welcome change, it was to be hoped.

Two men suddenly came into view, standing in a field by the roadside. There was something odd about them. They had guns under their arms and their features were nipped red by the cold. They smiled up at the coach as it passed and tugged their forelocks in salute.

It was their clothes that were odd! Not odd, just archaic. They were obviously part of the Dingley Dell scenery. Journey's end must be near.

Not many minutes later this was confirmed when the coach turned off the metalled surface into a real country lane, rutted and hollowed by the passage of vehicles in wet conditions. Now the ruts were frozen hard and the passengers in the coach got a real taste of the problems of travel a century and a half earlier as they were tossed and bounced against each other. Suzie seemed to enjoy it and even Leclerc smiled thinly as he returned Arabella to her own seat. It was, Arabella decided, merely an extra touch of the *or-then-tique* to impress people like Suzie.

They were probably very close to Dingley Dell now. She had caught a glimpse over to the left of a small cottage, now half ruined, but which might once have been a gatekeeper's house. Her theory was confirmed when very rapidly the lane's surface became perfectly level and the lane itself turned into a gravelled drive, curving round an island of shrubs at the centre of which was a magnificent holly tree, superbly jewelled with crimson berries. As the drive straightened out again, the guard's bugle sent another rousing fanfare to announce their coming and Arabella leaned out of the window to see where the drive was leading them.

Dead ahead at a distance of under a quarter of a mile stood a house, clearly visible in this clear air. It was a long spawling building, probably originally built according to the special needs of some eighteenth-century farming family rather than the architectural dogma of any age. Several long chimneys smoked welcomingly into the noontide air.

'We're arriving,' she said, returning her head to the inside of the coach.

'Let me see! Let me see!' cried Suzie, thrusting her expensively coiffured head out into the open air. *'Magnifique! Magnifique!'*

It was difficult to tell whether she was commenting on the house or on the figure who stepped forward from the ivy-wreathed porchway to greet them. A man of late middle age, portly but nimble, good will and welcome printed in every line of his broad, open face, he was an impressive enough figure in himself. But clothed in a blue coat, with bright buttons, corduroy breeches and top-boots, he was indeed magnificent.

'Step you down, step you down!' he cried. 'Be welcome to Dingley Dell! Wardle's my name and cheerful's my nature. Where's the steps? Joe! Joe! Wake that boy up, someone! There you are, Joe. Come on, boy, let down the steps.'

Out of the door behind him walked, or rather rolled, the tardy Joe. Arabella had rarely seen such a fat youth. His dimensions bordered on the grotesque even to his round red face under which the weight of his three chins served to keep his mouth perpetually agape. Arabella shuddered. If this was authenticity they could keep it. She had never liked the character of the fat boy much in Dickens' story, but his present incarnation was far worse than any mental image.

Joe let down the steps with a bad grace and was pushed aside by Wardle who offered a readily accepted hand to aid Suzie in her descent. Stephen Swinburne jumped down next and helped Arabella after him. Leclerc's slight insignificant figure came last.

'Ladies, gentlemen. You are welcome. Come into the house, we have a tall fire and a bowl of hot punch waiting to chase away the chill of your journey. Then straight to the table for dinner. We keep country hours here, dinner at noon, on the stroke. But we follow country pastimes too, so never fear for your appetites!'

Will he keep this up *all* the time? wondered Arabella.

She paused at the old oak doorway and glanced back at the coach down from which the coachman was passing the luggage to the unenthusiastic Joe. It really was beautiful. As she turned back to the house, a brief flash of light caught her eyes, as though up in the low wooded ridge which lay in a crescent to the east of the house a piece of glass had caught the heatless rays of the frosty-red sun.

Wardle had noticed too, of that she was sure, though there was no break in his welcoming flow. But once they were in the house, seated before the promised fire with a pretty red-cheeked maid (someone's part-casting was very good) helping them to a steaming spiced punch, Wardle begged their pardon and stepped outside again, ostensibly to oversee the unloading of their luggage. Arabella rose and strolled over to the low deep window. Outside she could see their host talking earnestly and rapidly to a small dark man wearing a groom's costume.

'Is it not wonderful, Miss Allen!' exclaimed Suzie, who had come up behind her. 'Just as I imagine it, yes?'

Arabella smiled at her and replied, 'Just.'

When she glanced out of the window again the groom had disappeared and a moment later Wardle re-entered the room.

'Your luggage is safely stowed and awaits you in your chambers,' he cried. 'Finish your punch, drink it all down, then we'll give you a few moments to get yourselves ready for dinner!'

'I do not think I shall dine so early,' murmured Leclerc with a hint of distaste. 'The journey has fatigued me. I should like to rest.'

'Rest! What is this rest?' demanded Suzie. 'You may rest, but I shall eat!'

'And what about you, Miss Allen?' enquired Stephen Swinburne.

'Oh, I shall eat. I was brought up never to miss a meal,' said Arabella.

Authenticity, she was glad to discover, did not extend to the plumbing and the decorators and designers had wisely made no attempt to retain the period atmosphere in her bathroom. She took Wardle at his word and had time for a quick shower only. Even then the great iron gong she had noticed at the foot of the stairs sounded before she was half dressed.

'There you are, Miss Allen!' said Wardle from the hall as

she descended. 'I thought you might have got lost. It's an old house, more complicated than it looks from outside.'

'I'm sure it is. It's certainly very beautiful.'

'Yes, it is. This way!'

He led her from the entrance hall down a long stone passage lit by small, square windows at intervals of three or four yards.

She paused at one of these which had a broken pane and looked out. Dark against the cold blue sky she could see the further horn of the crescent ridge she had noticed on her arrival. On this side of the house it looked closer, more menacing.

'You wouldn't think we were not much more than fifty miles from London,' said Wardle behind her.

'No,' she answered.

Distantly there sounded a dull noise like a paper bag not very strenuously burst, or rather two paper bags burst so closely together as to be almost inseparable. A surge of rooks rose from the trees on the ridge, cawing in protest.

'What was that?' she asked.

'Someone having a bit of sport with the rooks or perhaps one of my keepers bagging a brace of pheasant for supper,' said Wardle with a laugh. 'Come along, my dear. There's been a side of beef roasting in the kitchen all morning, but with Dingley Dell appetites, it could be all gone by the time you sit for dinner!'

The circling rooks were already returning to their perches as she turned away from the window. The intrusive and unexpected only caused the most momentary of diversions in their lives.

As Arabella entered the dining room and smiled at the circle of curious faces which turned to watch her, she wished it was a quality of living she could share.

2

*I'm not going to be shot in a wheelbarrow, for
the sake of appearances, to pleases anybody.*

MR. SAMUEL PICKWICK

'And last but not least, with his carver in his hand, is the man
who keeps us all right, our Mr. Boswell, known most fittingly
as Boz!'

'I'm pleased to meet you, Mr. Boswell,' said Arabella.

'Boz. It's in my contract that everyone calls me Boz. May
I help you to a slice of beef?'

'You may help me to two. The journey has given me an
appetite.'

A cool customer, thought Boswell. Not bad-looking.
Young, inexperienced, but looked as if she would learn fast.
If you didn't bed her in fifteen minutes you'd be hard pushed
to bed her at all. So, unless there was a way to have her between the syllabub and the cheese, he might as well not bother.

'Yet a slice for me, please,' commanded the huge woman on
his right.

'Certainly, Frau Himmelstor.'

Frau Cow. Fat Bitch. This was her third helping. She hadn't
even paused from eating as Arabella had been introduced
round the table. Himmelstor, though almost equally fond of

16

his food, had done the whole Teutonic courtesy bit, standing up, bowing from the waist, clicking his heels. The Swinburnes, who seemed to be having more difficulty talking with their newly arrived son than they would with a stranger on a train, had clearly welcomed the slight diversion. Young Stephen (Young? Nineteen? Twenty-one?) had brightened visibly.

The other guests at the long table, which could seat a couple of dozen at a pinch, had smiled and nodded. The Burtons, a pleasant round-faced couple with Yorkshire accents, had looked particularly friendly, but were rather too far down the table to engage in conversation. From the resumed buzz of talk after the round of introductions it was clear to Arabella's keen hearing that there were quite a number of foreigners present at the meal. There were no fixed places, but Wardle had escorted the newcomer to a seat next to the beef and Boswell.

'I like your costume,' said Arabella.

'Thank you, kind lady,' said Boswell, resuming his seat after the exertions of carving. 'The rule is that everyone dresses up for the party tonight and remains in period dress all through Christmas Day. We have a wide selection of suitable clothes and one of the maids is a dab hand with a needle if any adjustments need to be made.'

'I have something with me that I think may be all right for this evening,' said Arabella.

'Have you now? I must insist on the right of inspection. We can't have a false note being struck.'

She looked at him seriously.

'Then I would suggest you remember the *Papers* appeared in the thirties and were set some ten years earlier. The kind of lapels you're wearing didn't appear till after 1840. They should be rolled.'

Oh no! groaned Boswell inwardly. She's not going to be a smartie-pants, is she? It's bad enough without having an amateur expert about the place.

'You can pay too much attention to detail,' he said aloud. 'Don't you think?'

'I shouldn't have thought so. Not if you're Oscar Boswell, President-elect of the Dickens Circle and second youngest Fellow in the modern history of St. Sepulchre's College.'

'Good God! You're a policewoman!'

Arabella smiled.

'I always read dust-jacket blurbs. I thought your last book was superb.'

What a lovely smartie-pants it is! thought Boswell. Give us a kiss and I'll crown you Queen of the May.

Wardle, who had been urging a lugubrious footman to chase round with the wine and porter, took his seat opposite.

'That's why he's with us, Miss Allen. We need an expert and when we need something we go for the best. It's the only way in life! Eat up, Miss Allen, eat up. Boz, my boy, another slice of the beef for the lady.'

'No thank you,' said Arabella, but Wardle had already turned his attention from her and was on his feet again.

'Madame Leclerc! We have missed you!'

Suzie walked through the door, dressed in a tight-fitting electric blue catsuit.

Jackpot! thought Boswell.

'I am late? No? I ask your pardon. My husband is fatigued and will lie down.'

'Poor man,' breathed Arabella. Boswell shot her a sharp glance.

'Sit beside me then,' said Wardle, going forward. The footman stepped into his path and murmured into his ear. For a moment the smile faded from his face.

'Excuse me one moment, if you please. Sit you down. Boz, see to our new guest. The best of English beef for the fairest of French lilies.'

His heart did not seem altogether in the compliment and he hurried from the room.

''Allo,' said Suzie to Arabella with a friendly smile which included Boswell.

''Allo to you too,' said Boswell.

Mrs. Burton, the Yorkshirewoman, pushed her chair back and went over to the window.

'What's going on, love?' called her husband.

'I don't know,' she answered. 'I think there's been some kind of accident.'

Boswell stopped in mid-slice and moved swiftly to the

window, leaving the carver in the beef. After a moment Arabella followed him.

The window overlooked the main approaches to the house. The coach-and-four had disappeared. Approaching the house were the two gamekeepers who had greeted it along the road. They were pushing something before them.

Out of the front door came Wardle, who went to meet them. They all stopped and spoke together, then resumed the approach. As they neared the front door, it became apparent that what they were pushing was a ramshackle barrow of the type that gardeners use for collecting leaves and garden rubbish.

But the rubbish this one contained was a man.

Wardle backed carefully into the house, easing the barrow wheel over the doorstep. The man sprawled loosely, like a bonfire-night guy. Then one of the handles slipped a little and his head turned slowly towards the dining-room window. It looked almost like a deliberate movement.

But it was clear his eyes were seeing nothing.

'Who is it?' whispered Mrs. Burton in horror. No one replied at first.

'I saw him when we arrived,' said Arabella, suddenly penetrating the man's pale mask.

It was the dark-skinned groom Wardle had been talking to in front of the house.

The melancholy procession had now passed inside and they returned to the table. Most of the dozen or so guests present had risen or made some movement indicating interest, curiosity, concern. Only the elder Swinburne had remained in his seat with the indefinable air of one who does not go to see for himself but waits for his minions to return bearing reports. His wife, a pretty but rather sullen-looking woman much younger than her silvery-haired husband, did the reporting, while Stephen tucked into his dinner with undiminished appetite.

As did Arabella, Boswell was interested to see. And as Suzie intended to, she indicated with a smile, as soon as he finished slicing her beef.

The door opened and Wardle reappeared, eager to put

19

their minds at rest. Even if he had missed the onlookers at the window, which he hadn't, the atmosphere in the dining room would have sent signals down his host's antennae.

He was at once grave and reassuring.

'An accident, I'm afraid. One of the servants. He's had a nasty fall.'

'How melancholy!' sighed Suzie.

'Not badly injured, I hope,' said Swinburne suavely.

'Oh no. Cracked ribs perhaps. And shock. We're whipping him off to the Cottage Hospital the other side of the railway station. He'll enjoy his Christmas dinner as much as you, sir.'

Wardle was convincing. The jollity was back at full radiance now. Boswell caught Arabella's eye fleetingly. But the moment was enough to tell him she was thinking what he was thinking.

The man in the barrow would need more than a night in hospital to bring back his appetite.

'Where did he fall from?' asked Arabella.

'Oh the silly fellow was taking a stroll up the hill at the side of the house,' answered Wardle easily. 'There's a small quarry just before the trees begin and he must have strayed off the path to peer down. The frosty surface did the rest. So be careful, will you, my friends, on your post-prandial perambulations! If you want to slide, then slide you shall, but in good order and good company. The weather's been kind to us, there's a two-inch-thick sheet of ice on the Jockey Pond half a furlong behind the house, and we've got skates to fit all feet.'

'Do you skate, Miss Allen?' enquired Boswell.

'I can. But I don't think I will. Not today. A gentle stroll is more to my taste after a large meal.'

'If you think this is large, wait till tomorrow. Perhaps you'd like me to show you round the policies?'

'Policies?'

'Scots for the grounds. Veneration for a great English writer hasn't made me forget my origins.'

Arabella nodded thoughtfully.

'All right. If you wish.'

Boswell had had more enthusiastic receptions to his offers

than this, but he could see it would have to suffice. He smiled as he helped himself to the syllabub.

Half an hour later they exchanged greetings with the skating party which was moving off from the back of the house. It comprised seven or eight women but only a couple of men.

'So much for the stronger sex,' said Arabella, moving off to the right.

'Perhaps the stronger sex has better things to do,' said Boswell, raising his left eyebrow, a trick to which Arabella responded by raising her right even higher.

They plodded on in silence for a while, following a winding path which gradually began to steepen as it struck up towards the dark mane of trees on top of the crescent-shaped ridge. Halfway up, Arabella paused and Boswell came to a halt beside her. They glanced over to the house. They were already higher than the first-floor windows.

'Someone has been clearing the ground here,' said Arabella. Boswell glanced down the hillside. Beneath the whiteness of the frost it was evident that fire and scythe had been put to work and the stumps of once tall trees protruded bluntly like weather-rounded tombstones.

'So they have,' he said. 'Perhaps it was too handy for Peeping Toms, eh? You'd get a nice view into those bedrooms at the side. No *voyeurs* at Dingley Dell!'

'It should be Manor Farm, shouldn't it?' said Arabella, resuming her walk.

'That's right,' said Boswell, unsurprised now by her knowledge. 'Dingley Dell was the village. But Manor Farm doesn't mean much to most people. Only us experts.'

She ignored the gentle irony of his tone.

'Exactly what are you doing with your expertise here, Mr. Boswell?' she asked.

Now he did look surprised.

'Why, I'm giving advice, making suggestions, keeping things on the Dickensian straight and narrow.'

'Carving the roast beef, waiting at table and taking orders from Mr. Wardle,' added Arabella.

'He pays me well for it,' said Boswell with a shrug. 'My

21

Fellowship's not worth much and even superb books on Dickens don't make a fortune.'

They were almost at the trees now. The red-tiled roof of the house lay beneath them. Distantly they heard a scream of laughter which must have come from the skating party who were out of sight. Boswell looked with pleasure at the girl ahead of him as she glanced round. She showed no sign of discomfort from her exertions, but the frosty air had nipped her cheeks to a glowing ruddiness and the condensation from her breath had left her lips looking warm and moist.

'That must be the quarry over there,' she said suddenly, and turned off the path. Boswell was taken by surprise.

'Careful!' he cried. 'We don't want another accident.'

So saying, he stepped off the path himself, caught his foot in a tussock of grass and almost fell. By the time he recovered, the girl was at the edge of the quarry and peering in.

As quarries went, it was a pretty miniscule affair, hardly more than a harrowing of the hillside. At some time in the past, in the early days of the farm, it might have been a useful source of stone for walls and byres and other small structures. But it had obviously been long unused. The marks of the groom's descent through the ferns which grew out of the steep (though not perpendicular) sides were plain to see.

And speckled among the green of the leaves and the white of the frost were darker spots.

'He must have cut himself in the fall,' said Boswell. 'I'd prefer it if you wouldn't stand so near the edge.'

Arabella stepped back as though in compliance, then pointed to the ground at her feet.

'It looks as if he cut himself before he fell,' she said. 'Badly.'

The dark spots on the edge of the quarry almost formed a pool.

'Nose-bleed,' suggested Boswell, unconvincingly. She ignored him, peering up at the line of trees which fringed the ridges crest only a few yards away.

'Perhaps we should be getting back,' said Boswell.

'What? You don't call what we've done a walk?' retorted the girl, and began to move towards the trees.

The ground here was protected from the frost by the gnarled

22

old beeches whose branches, even leafless, were close-woven enough to provide an almost solid ceiling. Boswell lengthened his stride so that he overtook the girl who was moving slowly now, eyes intent on the ground. He came to a halt by one of the trees and leaned back against it, blowing into his cupped hands.

'Not so warm,' he said.

'Excuse me,' said Arabella.

'Sorry?'

'Excuse me. Would you mind moving? Your foot. There we are.'

She stopped and came up with a small cylinder of cardboard on a brass base, still bright despite having been pressed into the ground. Boswell glanced at it without interest.

'Quite the little jackdaw, aren't you? Shall we press on? Or go back?'

'If you like. I've seen enough up here,' said Arabella, turning away with an infuriating casualness. 'Thank you for your guidance.'

And shrieked, gently but genuinely, as she almost walked into a tall figure, dark against the low-dipping sun, carrying a long-barrelled shotgun which was pointed straight at her exquisitely slender waistline.

3

*Sound the gong, draw up the curtain, and enter
the two conspiraytors!*

MR. SAM WELLER

'Oh it's you, Mr. Boswell,' said the long gamekeeper with the overtight leggings. 'Sorry if I startled you, miss.'

He swung the gun through about two degrees so that it would merely remove most of her left rib-case if it went off. It was a small enough mercy, but it brought back Arabella's powers of speech.

'What the hell are you doing prowling around up here like an Indian?' she demanded indignantly.

'Sorry, miss,' the man repeated, 'but it *is* my job. You've got to move quietly when there's vermin about. I thought I might try for a few rooks. Oh, I see you've got one of my cartridge cases. Thanks. I don't like to litter up the country-side with them.'

Smiling, he plucked the case from Arabella's fingers, tipped his forehead and moved swiftly and silently away.

'Damn!' said Arabella, taking a pace after him.

Boswell caught her arm.

'What's the matter?' he said, amused. 'Has he stolen your little souvenir? Never mind, we'll get you another.'

'Not like that one you won't,' replied Arabella.

'What's so special about that one?'

She eyed him speculatively for a moment before answering.

'There can't be many 410 cartridges fired from twelve-bore guns.'

Boswell laughed again.

'Still more expertise! I've no idea what it means, but it sounds very impressive. Come on. First down the hill gets a broken leg!'

He was charmed by the ease with which she cast off her serious mood and, pushing him aside, cried, 'All right! Let's move!'

She shot into a five-yard lead, moving nimbly and sure-footedly ahead of him until she succumbed to the temptation to slide on the glistening grass and after a couple of yards fell back heavily on to the ground.

He bent over her anxiously. Her eyes were closed.

'Are you all right?' he asked, conscious of the stupidity of the traditional question.

She opened her eyes and looked at his worried face. Then she lifted her head slightly, put one hand to the back of his neck, pressed his face towards her and kissed him. It was a good kiss and she took her time.

Finished, she moved him gently aside, stood up and began dusting herself down.

'What was that for?' he asked politely.

'Like Lizzie Borden said to the jury, it seemed the only thing to do in the circumstances,' she said with a grin. 'But don't let it give you ideas. Let's get on down, shall we?'

It's too late, thought Boswell as he watched her step sedately before him down the path. It's given me all kinds of ideas already. That bromide they put in the Fellows' port must have passed through my system.

As they reached the house, the rural silence was shattered by the roar of a tractor engine.

'Not very Dickensian that,' grinned Arabella.

'No. I'll go and have a word. Excuse me. See you later.'

He went quickly round to the front of the house just in time to see a large tractor coming down the hillside towards the barn which adjoined the stables and coach house about fifty yards from the main building. Behind it, being dragged along at the end of a thirty-foot length of chain, was a lopped tree-trunk.

The tractor came to a halt by the barn and Boswell approached.

'Not today, Harry,' he shouted to the driver, a sullen-looking man in a dirty cloth cap. 'Not while the guests are here.'

'It's you as wanted the hillside cleared,' grunted the man.

'Yes. But no more, eh? And be careful when you put the tractor away to leave a bit of space. We've got a band coming this evening and they'll want to put their van in the barn. O.K.?'

Without waiting for an answer, Boswell returned to the house. The man Harry watched him enter, then spat. He laboriously unhooked the chained tree from the tractor, but did not get back into the driving seat.

'They can have all the bloody room they like,' he muttered, climbing on his push-bike and setting off grimly down the drive.

Boswell had already forgotten the incident as he re-entered Dingley Dell. The skating party had not yet returned and the hotel was very quiet. He made his way quickly up the stairs, along a narrow corridor which terminated in what seemed to be a solid oak door. Only an expert carpenter with time to look closely could have detected that this wood was by no means of the same ancient vintage as the rest of the house. It was in fact a veneer over solid steel.

Boswell did not try the handle or even knock. He merely ran his forefinger lightly under the upper lip of the bottom panel. After a moment the door was opened by a gross figure who stood there silently, making no effort to let him in.

'All well, Joe?' asked Boswell.

The Fat Boy nodded.

'Is Colley in there with you?'

Again the nod.

'Right. Send him up to my room with Miss Arabella Allen's file, will you? Right away.'

He turned, then stopped.

'For God's sake, cheer up, Joe. You're supposed to add local colour, not bloody gloom! Don't forget. I want that file as quickly as possible.'

This time he moved off without hesitation. Behind him the door swung silently to.

Down by the pond, the fun was in full swing. Suzie Leclerc, gorgeous in a figure-hugging ski-suit, span and glided in a series of graceful loops and turns. Frau Himmelstor, grosser than ever in a totally style-less fur coat, moved doggedly round the outermost circle of the ice, content simply to move forward but displaying a competence which many of the others envied.

A brazier filled with hot coals had been set up by the pond, and on the metal sheet lying on top of it chestnuts cracked and popped. Suzie hopped elegantly on to the bank and teetered on her skates to the brazier, balancing herself when she reached it against the shoulder of the sturdy countryman in charge of the chestnuts.

'Warm work, missus,' he said with a grin. 'What's your pleasure? Chestnut? Or a drop of the master's punch?'

'Both please.'

The man bent down to the small urn of rich brown liquid which rested against the brazier, and Suzie, deprived of her support, nearly slipped.

'Hello,' said Stephen Swinburne, one of the only three men with the party.

''Allo, Monsieur Swinburne. May I lean on you while I stand? I wish to skate again soon, so I have retained the skates.'

She didn't wait for a reply but transferred her weight to his shoulder, pinning his arm to his side with her breasts. He looked at her warily but made no objection.

'This is good, is it not?' said Suzie, with a gesture that included the pond, the weather, the landscape and the punch which was being placed in her hand.

'Yes,' said Stephen. 'It's funny, though. I would have thought there'd have been more men.'

Suzie eyed him closely.

27

'You do not feel safe with so many women?'

'No, it's not that,' protested Stephen.

'Or are you, what is it they say? Gay? No,' she said, pressing herself a little harder against him. 'You do not feel gay.'

Stephen ignored the comment.

'I just meant that it's usually the men who are active and hearty while the women like a cosy fireside chat.'

'Active and hearty? Active, yes. But I am not hearty! Some of the others, perhaps yes.'

She glanced to where a little gaggle of middle-aged women were being girlishly jolly as one of Wardle's young men tried to initiate them into the mysteries of skating. He was using Frau Himmelstor as an object lesson as she went sailing majestically by.

'And her, the German, she is not hearty. They are not a race with much of heart.'

'Frau Cow, you mean?' asked Stephen.

'Who? Ah yes! Frau Cow. That is good!'

'It's not original,' confessed the youth. 'I overheard Mr. Boswell say it after dinner. But the husband, I've christened him Herr Bear. That's original.'

'Good also,' murmured Suzie. 'Mr. Boswell. An interesting man, don't you think?'

'Very. I've read some of his books. He's a fine scholar.'

'I was not thinking of his books.'

'Where is Monsieur Leclerc this afternoon?' asked Stephen suddenly.

The question never got answered. Suddenly, as though with Teutonic thoroughness she had been keeping an exact check of her revolutions and had reached the appointed number, Frau Cow turned sharply and headed across the centre of the pond towards the bank where the brazier stood. The ice creaked protestingly, then, almost precisely in the middle, it let out a grating, crackling shriek; cracks zig-zagged frantically away from the huge woman, jagged panes of ice rose momentarily into the air and she sank slowly, steadily, into the water until it reached her chest. Everyone else had scrambled on to the bank at the first sound of disaster. There were one or two cries of dismay, but these died quickly away in the face of the German woman's own apparent indifference to the situation. For a long moment everyone stared in silence at the bright circle of ice from the centre of which Frau Himmelstor, seemingly oblivious to the bitterly cold water lapping her bosom, stared stolidly back. Finally she spoke, not loud nor in agitation, but clearly, rather commandingly.

'*Zur Hilfe, bitte*,' she said.

Such an unpleasant eventuality had not, it seemed, been ignored. The chestnut-roaster and the skating instructor rapidly manœuvred into position over the ice two long ladders which were lying amongst some nearby trees. Nimbly they made their way out over them to the sunk woman and hauled her out. The ice creaked and groaned threateningly, but no more cracks appeared and the woman was soon being helped to the safety of the bank.

Here there was some debate as to what was best to do with her—remove her sodden clothing here, subjecting her to the freezing air, or get her back to the house as quickly as possible.

Frau Cow herself said nothing, drank very rapidly about a pint of the hot punch, chewed a couple of chestnuts, then brought the debate to a close by marching determinedly away towards Dingley Dell.

Nearly everybody followed and soon Suzie and Stephen were left alone by the brazier.

'Disasters are like omelettes,' opined Suzie, looking after the departing crowd. 'Best served up fresh.'

'It's spoiled the skating,' said Stephen.

'It's true,' said Suzie.

She leaned all her weight on the youth's shoulder and began taking off her skates.

'What are we to do instead?' she asked softly, dropping the first skate to the ground.

'I thought I might go for a walk,' he said uncertainly.

Suzie laughed and released the other skate.

'Why not?' she said. 'But first, let us see if Frau Cow has left us any punch. Then we shall try how well you walk, *mon ami*!'

There was trouble at the station too. The last train of the day had gone leaving two passengers for the Dingley Dell coach, a woman in her late thirties and an elderly man whom she addressed as 'uncle' and who obviously felt his age and relationship entitled him to be embarrassingly irritated.

'Come along, come along,' he said, thrusting his head out of the coach window and brandishing at the driver the rough-hewn oak stick on which he leaned heavily as he walked. 'I don't particularly care to travel in this archaic vehicle and the less time I have to spend in it, the better.'

'Sorry, sir,' said the driver. 'There should have been another passenger. A Mr. Bennett. You didn't see anything of him, did you?'

'How should I know?' said the old man testily. 'The train was full of people, most of them very sensibly making their way *home* for Christmas instead of to some cranky, gimmicky hotel.'

'Uncle, please!' said the woman.

'He was middle-aged, small, dark-haired, with a moustache,' said the driver, consulting the sheaf of papers he had in his hand.

'No, I'm sorry,' said the woman. 'And I'm sure he didn't get off.'

'Thank you, Mrs. Hislop,' said the driver. 'Must have missed the train.'

'Best be moving, Alf,' said the guard. 'Want to use the daylight, don't you?'

They glanced up at the rapidly declining sun. Night came early and quickly at this time of year and though it was still mid-afternoon, dusk was not far away. To the north there was an ominous build-up of dark grey cloud obscuring the pale blue of the winter sky. Whatever the clouds carried was too far away to bother them on their journey back, but they were already nibbling at the fringes of the sun.

'Right, let's be off,' said the driver, climbing up on his box. The guard made sure the doors were fast, hauled himself up behind and set his key-bugle to his lips. But before he could play his usual fanfare there was an interruption.

'Hey! Wait for me!'

30

From behind the small cluster of buildings which comprised the small unmanned station a man had appeared. He ran towards the coach, waving. He was tall, fair-haired, with a fresh, open face. He wore a sheepskin jacket and carried a large tartan grip. And he was smiling widely.

'You're for Dingley Dell? You got to be with this outfit. Hey, I like it,' he said with a soft American accent.

He walked round the coach, smiling up at the guard and driver. His smile was not returned.

'Can I help you, sir?' asked the driver.

'Well, you can take me to the hotel, I guess,' said the man.

'Do you have a reservation, Mr.—er . . . ?'

'Sawyer. Why yes. In a manner of speaking.'

'What manner of speaking would that be, sir?' asked the driver. 'You don't seem to appear on my list anywhere.'

'I can explain that,' said the American, opening the coach door.

'What on earth's happening now?' demanded the old man.

The driver climbed down and looked enquiringly at the American, who smiled again.

'You mean you would like me to explain now? And if I don't satisfy you, what then? You leave me stuck *here*?'

He waved round at the deserted scene.

'There's a village just around that corner, sir,' said the driver. 'Now if you don't mind . . .'

'OK. This guy I know, now he *did* have a reservation, but something's come up and he can't make it. So I thought as long as I'm footloose and with nowhere special to go at Christmas, I might as well try a slice of the old-fashioned kind of English hospitality. Which is what I'm getting *now*?'

'Your friend's name?' pursued the driver stolidly.

'Bennett,' said Sawyer. 'Peter Bennett.'

The driver looked up at the guard, who shrugged non-committally.

'When is this contraption going to move?' demanded the old man.

'It *is* getting rather cold,' said Mrs. Hislop.

'Right, sir,' said the driver, making up his mind. 'You'd better hop in. I'll put your grip on the roof.'

'That's OK, driver. I'll hang on to it,' said Sawyer, stepping into the coach. 'Don't you stop for any Indians!'

'All snug? Then off we go!'

He shook out the reins; the horses, impatient of standing waiting in the cold, bounded forward eagerly, the guard released the butt of the Walther PPK which his hand had been resting on for the past two minutes and once more took up his bugle.

The notes stretched poignantly away behind him as the coach rattled forward into the gathering dusk.

They fell gently on the ears of the sole inhabitant of the little ticket office which British Rail's penny-pinching frugality had closed down. Passengers for the hotel were privileged to be dropped here at all. Someone somewhere must have influence.

The man in the office, whose name was, and had been for many years, solely Jimmy, was unsurprised and unimpressed by privilege. He looked with pleasure at the gift of two rabbits and a pheasant which had just been presented to him. It had been the act of a gentleman, though there had been a moment when some kind of most ungentlemanly action had seemed possible. But it had passed.

He bent down and pulled up a loose floorboard. He had been right, he thought, scratching his free-sprouting ginger beard. Someone had moved it.

From the depths he pulled up a waterproof jacket. It felt heavy. It took him a few seconds to find the shotgun barrel. He let it drop back into the pocket.

Quickly but carefully he replaced the jacket under the floor. Privilege he didn't given a rap for. But with some people and matters he did not care to interfere.

Besides he owed something for the rabbits and pheasant. He wrapped them up carefully in newspaper, tucked them under his ragged coat and went off down the road, whistling.

It was nice some people remembered it was Christmas

4

It's—it's—only a gentleman, ma'am.
MR. SAMUEL PICKWICK

Arabella knew she was being watched.

She had felt a vague uneasiness since re-entering her room after her walk, but had been unable to pin it down. In the end she made up her mind it was merely the effect of the odd collection of small incidents which seemed to have taken place since her arrival, plus the fatigue of the journey and her walk. A pleasant soak in a hot bath, she decided, was the answer. But first she picked up the house telephone, an anachronism which even the brass-mounted receiver could not conceal.

'Reception,' said a bland, featureless voice. Probably male.

'Arabella Allen here,' she said. 'I was wondering, the man who got hurt in the fall, how is he?'

There was a short pause.

'Oh, he's very well, thank you, Miss Allen.'

'Good. I was quite concerned. Would he like a visitor, do you think? If he's in bed, he'll probably be bored to tears and I'm sure the staff must be very busy at the moment.'

Another pause.

'That's kind of you, Miss Allen, but in fact he's no longer

33

here. Mr. Wardle insisted that Custer, that's his name, should be driven to our nearest hospital for a thorough check-up. You can't be too careful, can you?'

'I'm not sure about that. Thank you,' said Arabella, replacing the receiver. She stood by the table for a moment, then with a shake of her head she started getting undressed.

By the time she had stripped down to her bra and pants, she knew for certain she was being watched. A year in Africa, living rough, had familiarised her with the feeling of being under constant scrutiny. No one could live and move in the bush without being aware of dozens of pairs of unseen eyes watching at any given moment. Curious, wary, indifferent, the gazes touched you and moved on, or you moved on. You became used to them. But when the scrutiny was more intense, when you and you alone were the object of it, when it was purposeful, assessing, or menacing, you recognised its touch as something out of the ordinary.

This was what Arabella felt now. The only question was, where was the watcher?

Clearly it was the act of undressing which had made his vibrations so strongly to be felt. She went into the bathroom and turned on the water. When she returned to the bedroom she paused in the door and unhooked her bra, trying to catch the further intensifying of feeling this would almost certainly cause.

The window seemed the obvious viewpoint, but it looked out on to the hillside up which she and Boswell had climbed and she knew there was no cover for a watcher there. In any case, it felt nearer, stronger than that.

She tossed the bra on to the bed, a casual movement, but her eyes were triangulating every square inch of the room and her mind was working furiously to check and correlate data. Notions of two-way mirrors, eyeholes in paintings and secret passages behind the wainscotting were considered and discarded.

There was something frightening but at the same time rather exciting in this blind-man's-buff striptease, she thought, as she lay back on the bed and began to ease off her pants.

Then she had it. In the ceiling panels, above the ornate

pseudo-candelabra, a knot-hole that wasn't. Nothing so start-ling as an actual eye peering whitely down at her, in fact no real evidence at all. But she knew. And, knowing now where the watcher was, there was no need to give him the pleasure of the full strip-show.

Pants resting on her hips, she rolled off the bed and warmed herself in front of the glorious open fire which was one area in which Dingley Dell went in for complete authenticity. She took her time. No need for the whole show, but no need either to let him see he was detected. *Him?* Certainly. Or a very queer *her*.

The bathroom she felt quite certain was not overlooked. This she was very glad of as she slid luxuriatingly into the scented water. There were some things she did not care to do under supervision.

She took her time, but when she came out again the eye was still there. So she quickly dressed and though not at all hungry descended to the parlour, where, her hotel brochure told her, tea and toasted muffins would be available for those who found the gap between dinner and supper too long.

The parlour presented an interesting spectacle. A long pleasantly proportioned room, it displayed a pleasing and effective gradation from Dickensian kitchen at one end to early Victorian parlour at the other. A fine Christmas tree, beauti-fully decorated, stood here, but the kitchen end was the main centre of activity.

There was a huge fireplace in which there glowed wickedly a huge fire. A large brass kettle sang merrily on a hob. The floor immediately surrounding the fire was of red-brick on which the embers and sparks which occasionally popped out died away harmlessly. The walls were decorated with several hunting whips, two or three bridles and an old rusty blunder-buss, with an inscription below it intimating that it was loaded. A fine grandfather clock stood in the corner.

A tray loaded with muffins and a cool stone platter of superbly yellow butter were laid out for the attention of any who wanted them. It was a do-it-yourself arrangement and half a dozen toasting forks, all of them at least four feet in length, had been provided. They looked dangerous weapons in the hands of the ladies of the skating party who were jostling for position in front of the fire and at the same time excitedly discussing Frau Himmelstor's recent immersion.

'It's like a scene from the *Inferno*, isn't it?' said Boswell.

She didn't even glance round, but replied as though she knew he had come silently in behind her.

'I suppose it is,' she answered. 'The Christmas tree's a bit of a bloomer, isn't it? That was post-Albert, surely?'

'Do you fancy a muffin?' he asked politely, ignoring her quibble.

Now she turned.

'It's called crumpet in my part of the world. No, I don't think so. Crumpet is notoriously bad for the figure.'

Your part of the world. And what part is that, Arabella Allen? thought Boswell, bringing back to his mind the single sheet of photostat foolscap he had been perusing for the last half-hour.

SUBJECT: Arabella Allen: b. February 1st, 1945.

That seemed about right.

Father—Michael Allen, milkman, of 120, Forest Road, Selby, Yorks. Deceased.

Mother—Eunice Allen. Deceased.

An orphan. Always convenient, that. There was no doubt whatsoever that Mike Allen the Selby milkman had lived and loved and been popular and doubtless done at least some of the extraordinary things milkmen are alleged to do. And his wife Eunice doubtless sat at home wondering who he was doing them with. But she'd had her daughter to look after. For a while.

Subject's parents died in motor accident, November 1952.

Subject brought up by her uncle, Samuel Allen, plumber and fitter, of 70A, Ashburton Grove, Leeds 6, until 1955 when he emigrated to South Africa. Subject taken into care by local authority.

Sad that. Left all alone in the world while selfish uncle went off to make his fortune. Which apparently he had done.

1958 Samuel Allen sends for subject to join him in Johannesburg where he had built up a substantial plumbing business.

Three years. Quick work. Perhaps all that cheap labour helped. Though did they let black fitters handle fitments in which white men, or worse, women, might bathe, or wash, or defecate?

1961 South Africa leaves the Commonwealth. Samuel Allen surrenders his British passport. Subject retains hers and returns to England. Undertakes course of secretarial training at a London business school. Financed by her uncle until she finishes the course and starts to work.

Nice guy. Easing off his conscience for those years he left her by herself. Important years. But not as important as the next three years in South Africa.

Boswell recalled the photographs in the file. Two of them were old. One was a blow-up from a larger picture of a group of young girls in school uniform. The other showed the same girl staring like a stoat-tranced rabbit into the camera. Obviously a passport picture.

The others were new, large, glossy. Clearly Arabella. Arabella striding happily out of the door of the large office block in which she worked. Arabella feeding the ducks in St. James's Park. Arabella entering the front door of her apartment block, her head half turned as if somehow she had momentarily become aware of the well-hidden cameraman distantly sighting his telescopic lens.

The gap hadn't bothered him before. There had been a careful check, of course. But there had seemed no reason of any kind for doubting that this pale, serious, rather buck-toothed girl was the same as this radiant, smiling, confident young woman. Not that there was any reason now. But since meeting her the image of successful career girl on holiday had become blurred at the edges.

His mind turned to the file again.

First job, secretary to a minor executive of Cerberus Chemicals Corporation. Her talents rapidly spotted. Rapid rise to the General Manager's office. No evidence of extramural duties—promotion seemed based purely on merit. 1968 Subject made Personal Assistant to the International Director. Many trips abroad. Subject spends any long holiday she takes in South Africa with her uncle. Last year on receipt of news of Samuel Allen's death in sailing accident subject quit her job with CCC and returned to South Africa for an extended stay to sort out his affairs. Returned to UK via overland route, driving herself, and camping in the bush. Long periods of no contact. Arrived UK July.

That should explain her acquaintance with shotguns. Only a fool would drive alone through the heart of Africa without a gun. And she did not strike him as a fool.

Nor, he thought, watching her efficiently extract a teapot from the midst of the gossiping women, did she strike him as a girl who would be content to do nothing but live in comfort on a rich uncle's legacy. Which, according to her file, was what she had been doing since her return, despite substantial and flattering offers from her former employers at CCC.

He sighed deeply. This was always the trouble. Reports seemed deep, all-inclusive, well researched, but so often they were done at a distance and when you met the subject they began to look threadbare. At this stage in the game, Christmas Eve with only two days to go, it had hardly seemed worth requesting additional probes. But he had done it none the less. It was an old rule known as 'covering yourself'. Not even the oldest, most moth-eaten Fellows of St. Sepulchre's failed to observe this rule. It would be nice to get back, for all that. At least there the violence was all cerebral and the only real weapons were words.

Someone plucked at his sleeve. It was Joe, grotesque in his tights and short jacket.

'Nothing wrong upstairs, Joe?' he asked, worried.

'No. I've just been relieved. The afternoon coach has just arrived and I was wanted for the local colour bit.'

'So?'

'So there's someone on it as oughtn't to be. He says his name's Sawyer. He sounds like a Yank.'

'Jesus Christ! What the hell were Alf and Dave thinking of!'

Boswell's further expressions of annoyance were brought to a halt by the entrance of Wardle and the newcomers.

'Room at the fire there! Room at the fire for wayworn

travellers! You're just in time for muffins and tea. Mind you, at Dingley Dell you're always in time for something! Joe, my boy, off you trot and fetch more muffins and lots of butter. Quick as you can, and don't be stopping to eat any on the way!'

It took a very keen auditor to detect the undercurrent of concern in Wardle's stream of joviality. Boswell had no difficulty at all.

He moved over to join the newcomers.

'Here's our Mr. Boswell, our resident expert. He keeps us all right, watches that we don't drop too many anachronisms. This is Mrs. Hislop. Mrs. Hislop's uncle, Mr. Bloodworth's here too, but he felt the strain of the journey a bit and has gone up to bed. And this is Mr. Sawyer.'

'Pleased to meet you, Mr. Boswell. That's a crazy rig you're wearing. Do we all get to wear something like that?'

'You'll find a suit will be placed in your wardrobe in time for the ball tonight,' said Wardle. 'Mr. Sawyer's a friend of Mr. Bennett, who unfortunately wasn't able to come.'

'And I was more than happy to take up his reservation. Boy, I just know I'm going to enjoy myself here!'

Sawyer's face split in a broad infectious grin and his eyes sparkled as he glanced around the room. He caught Arabella's eye and winked appreciatively at her. She scanned him critically for a moment, then, still deadpan, winked back.

Boswell was surprised to find himself annoyed.

'Tell me, Mr. Sawyer,' he said, 'Which variety are you, the American or English?'

'You've lost me, Mr. Boswell.'

'Well, Mark Twain or Dickens? Tom or Bob? We have to be sure of our literary antecedents here.'

'Oh, I'm with you! Well, you might say both, really. I'm Bob, sure enough, which fits me into the Pickwick picture if I recall rightly. But my full name is Robert E. Lee Sawyer which puts me splash down in the Mississippi.'

'I see,' said Boswell, fighting to control the waves of antipathy he felt surging inside him. 'Like a Colossus, you straddle two worlds.'

'Mr. Boswell,' said Sawyer coldly, though his smile lost

39

none of its charm, 'I generally straddle just whoever and whatever it takes my fancy to straddle. And at the moment I feel like straddling this fire and toasting myself a dozen of those little muffins. Excuse me.'

He turned away to the fire, helped himself to the muffin on the end of a fork held by a badly bleached matron, bit into it, smacked his lips, took the fork, kissed her hand and began toasting on his own account.

'What do you think?' asked Wardle.

'He's being checked?'

'Too true. But it'll take time. It *is* Christmas Eve. God, he's too blatant not to be true!'

'It's a technique. But if he's used it before, he'll be known.'

'What about Bennett? He was OK, wasn't he?'

Boswell shrugged.

'They're all OK till you find out different. But he's our only lead, anyway. That's where they'll start. By the way, how's Frau Cow?'

'Fine. I got word in to Himmelstor. He just grunted, it seems.'

'That figures. She really is his wife, which is more than you can say for most of the rest.'

Wardle shrugged in his turn.

'In the national interest . . . *dulce et decorum est* . . .'

'Yes? My Latin doesn't have the verb you want!'

Wardle grunted.

'I'd better go and be jolly. Oh God, here comes old man Bloodworth. Why couldn't the silly old sod go to sleep for an hour? We can do without a heart attack just now. Oh, Mrs. Hislop, here's your uncle. Mr. Bloodworth, sir! Come you in and join us. Be welcome! Tea and muffins at your service!'

'Muffins! Never touch the things. Give me heartburn. Where's my niece? I don't like being left by myself in a strange place!'

Boswell looked sympathetically at Mrs. Hislop. He brought her file to mind. She was a widow and her uncle had been living with her for about eighteen months since his retirement. Boswell suspected the previous Christmas had been such a

40

disaster that she had resolved to try an hotel this year. He wished them both luck.

She moved towards the old man, who leaned breathlessly on his stick in the doorway, and Boswell could now see down to the fire. Sawyer was still there, being very much at his ease among the ladies.

Beside him was Arabella, who turned her face away as Boswell looked. But not before Boswell got a clear view of her.

Not even the baking heat and the ruddy glow from the dancing flames could conceal the fact that she was as pale as death. As though she had looked into the shifting patterns of the fire and seen some strange hieroglyphs from another world.

5

Wery desperate ch'racter, your wash-up. He attempted to rescue the prisoners and assaulted the officers; so we took him into custody . . .

MR. GRUMMER

All over the country people were preparing to enjoy themselves on Christmas Eve. This was the night of the full house. Pubs, ballrooms, private parties—all would be packed as man, the lonely animal, went on one of his recurring 'togetherness' sprees. Even vicars, priests, ministers and pastors, generally the first to suffer when the alternatives of pleasure and promiscuity are placed before their flocks, were expecting the seating capacities of their churches, chapels, temples and tin huts to be strained.

But there were those who had to work, Christmas Eve or no. Many would be working at just those places where their fellows were enjoying themselves. They might even enjoy their work.

But some worked alone.

The man searching Bennett's flat had been on his way to a party when the instructions came. At least he had been on his way to pick up the girl he was taking with him to the party.

He had planned to call on her early, wanting to start the night the way he was certain it would end.

Then the phone had rung.

He wasn't sure whether he wanted to find anything important or not. If he found something connecting Bennett and Sawyer it might make everybody happy and get him to the party on time. On the other hand it might just land him with a follow-up job.

Whereas if he found *nothing* . . . he was just as likely to be sent somewhere else till he found *something*.

But *nothing* was just what he was finding at the moment.

He sat down and lit a cigarette, something he would never normally dream of doing on a job. Tonight was different. Usually he took a pride in his work. But tonight he resented it. Bennett, he was increasingly certain, had gone off somewhere else quite happily. Probably a bird turning up out of the blue, ready and willing for a bit of wassail. The Dingley Dell reservation had been condescendingly flung to Robert E. Lee Sawyer. Mad for pseudo-culture like all these bastard Americans. It all fitted.

But he had to keep on looking.

'Bennett, Bennett,' he moaned softly as he stood up. 'You lucky sod. I wish I was in your shoes right now!'

One by one he began to remove the books from the bookshelf.

Peter Bennett's left shoe was at that moment bobbing in the shallows of the Thames Estuary just off Southend. But it would have been difficult for the reluctant searcher of his flat to be in it, as it was still occupied by a foot.

'Algie,' said Mary Swinburne, poking petulantly at a wisp of hair which would not stay in place.

'Yes, my love,' replied Algernon Swinburne with the affectionate complacency of one who knows that his knighthood is safely stowed in the New Year Honours list.

'It sounds a bit old-fashioned Woman's Mag-ish, but I *am* rather worried about Stephen.'

'My dear, if you're going to worry about the boy when he's

43

here with us, what will you do when, as for ninety-five per cent of the time nowadays, he is not?'

His wife gave up the curl and admired instead the very becoming Victorian evening gown she wore.

'This dress was my grandmother's,' she said.

'You tell everyone that in case they think it was your mother's,' said Swinburne, debating internally whether to enjoy the one cigar a day his doctor allowed him here at his ease or wait till he went below, where he might be interrupted.

'I saw him come in with that French *thing.*'

'Hard to believe as it seems, my love, she really *is* Leclerc's wife.'

Mary Swinburne snorted her disbelief, didn't quite get it right, and snorted again.

'I doubt if it makes much difference!'

'Stephen is nearly twenty,' said her husband patiently. 'He has long since discovered self-abuse does not grow hair on his hands. He may or may not have discovered that partner-sex does not grow hair on his chest. Madame Leclerc may well be a necessary step in his education.'

Mary Swinburne turned from the mirror to look at her husband.

'You know, Algie,' she said, 'I have a great respect for your intelligence. You've gone far and I don't delude myself that I have played any significant role in your progress.'

He made a deprecating little noise which she cut off by continuing.

'Apart from the psychological boost my enthusiastic reception of your advances must have given you. Perhaps that's been the trouble. You see the problems of the young purely in terms of sex. Is it good? Is it bad? Is it experienced? Is it naïf? But I assure you, when I say I'm worried about Stephen, I am *not* talking about sex. He thinks as well as feels. He's got a social conscience, what you would call "politics". I had a talk with him when he was unpacking. He still talks to me, though he feels precious little loyalty towards you or your job. But fortunately I do, so listen to what I say. And put that cigar away. You'll want it later.'

'What *are* you worried about, my dear?'

44

By the time she had finished telling him, the room was blue with cigar smoke.

'How was your afternoon?' asked Leclerc.

'Interesting. And yours?'

'Cautious.'

He stepped back from the mirror in front of which he had been adjusting his white neck-stock.

'Do I have to wear this absurd costume? These tights. They are disgusting.'

Suzie touched her own beautiful bare shoulders complacently.

'Nonsense. They show you to advantage. You have a fine leg.'

'The leg I do not mind. The boy, how was he?'

'Cautious. Surprisingly so.'

'Pah!' said Leclerc with elegant scorn. 'Swinging Britain is just another Anglican myth. The English achieve nothing. They merely take in the world with their deceits.'

Suzie looked at him quizzically.

'I wonder, Jules, if you are the right man for this job.'

'Not the right. The only one. You think the boy knows?'

'Oh yes. I'm sure of it.'

'Good. Work on him tonight. At the moment he is a danger. Once we have him in the open he becomes a weapon.'

'He's not a fool.'

'Nor are you, my dear. He thinks you are my mistress?'

'Of course.'

'Good. Enjoy yourself, my dear.'

'You also, Jules. But in those tights, not too much, eh?'

'You are well enough for this, *Liebchen*?'

'Why should I not be? A little water! They do not have winters here, they have early springs. At home the ice would be a metre, two perhaps.'

'We are not so young now,' said Himmelstor. 'This uniform it becomes me, yes?'

'Yes. You look good, Udo. The old-fashioned clothes, they suit you.'

45

'Some of them. Well, today has been hard for both of us. The difference is that your cold water was English, mine was French.'

He wheezed mightily at his joke and filled his cigar case with huge black cigars.

'Always the French. Why are they so distrustful?'

'Help me with this sword. They are a race who thrive on distrust. They invite betrayal because they enjoy it. They get more pleasure in bed if they imagine the woman's husband is hiding underneath.'

He bit off the end of a cigar and moved the butt of tobacco appreciatively around his mouth for a moment.

'Historically,' he concluded, 'it has often been our national duty to see that our neighbours are not disappointed.'

He spat the cigar butt expertly into a waste-paper basket.

'But tonight we enjoy ourselves. Like at home. It is good that we go into the past. For the English too once knew how to enjoy themselves before they forgot they also are Germans.'

Robert E. Lee Sawyer lay on his bed and puffed smoke-rings at the ceiling. He hadn't yet started changing into his ball costume. He looked at it again and laughed. He was very happy. He thrived on expertise, he adored touches of subtlety.

For instance, they hadn't just bothered to search his grip, they had unpacked it for him. Real service! All his papers (which were unequivocally in order) were ranged neatly on the dressing table, and there was a polite note saying some of his clothes had become rather creased in the journey and had been removed for pressing.

Better still was the suit he had been given for the ball. As they had been expecting Mr. Bennett, whose dimensions differed from Mr. Sawyer's in almost every particular, they were sorry but the only costume they could offer him was rather eclectic, if not to say eccentric, in composition.

He looked again at the heavy jacket, the tight drabs and the awkward-looking boots.

One thing was certain: whoever wore that was not going to have an easy time wandering freely round the house.

There was a knock at the door and a maid entered carrying

his newly-pressed clothes. She was a pretty, red-cheeked buxom girl with an inviting gleam in her eye. He raised himself up on one elbow and looked consideringly at her. It was very possible that she was specially provided by the management. Not that that bothered him. His motto was, first saddle your gift horse then look it in the mouth. But the night was young, there was much to do, and when it came down to it, he did prefer to break in his own mounts.

'Thanks,' he said, and relaxed on to the bed once more, not even bothering to watch the girl leave.

Now, Arabella Allen. He really fancied digging his spurs into her noble flanks if time permitted.

It could be a busy Christmas.

Arabella was not conscious of Sawyer's lusty thoughts. If she had been, they would not have bothered her. She was aware of her attractions and the physiological effects they had on men. But she was wise enough to relate male desire to its general cause and not be over-flattered by any image of herself as a specially endowed source. She knew many women more beautiful than herself. She also knew many who were plainer and yet generated a much greater sexuality than she did—or wished to do.

So lustful thoughts did not bother her, nor lustful looks either, generally speaking. But this eye in the ceiling, overlooking her like a *voyeur* god, was beginning to get on her nerves.

She postponed changing as long as possible, sitting in front of the bedroom fire with her dressing gown wrapped round her. To take her superb white gown into the bathroom would be a clear statement that she knew about the watcher. But it was either that or carry on with the pretence of ignorance.

Distantly she heard someone shout. And again. She went to the door and opened it slightly.

'Joe! Joe! Drat that boy! Sleeping again, I don't doubt! Joe, boy, where are you.'

It was Wardle, speaking his lines again. But this time she thought she recognised a note of real irritation in them.

47

She turned back into the room and felt at once the watcher had gone.

The two things came together in the same instant. Wardle shouting, the eye disappearing. Joe. It must be Joe.

The thought made her shudder. To be spied on by anybody was bad enough. But the Fat Boy, that made her skin feel dirty.

But if it was Joe there was the chance of a bit of back-tracking here. She had already made a casual tour of the first floor of the house without being able to work out how one got to the attic floor above. There was a whole wing sealed off by doors marked *Private*. She assumed this was where the offices and the staff quarters were situated and it seemed most likely that the entrance to the upper reaches of the house was contained here. But it would be useful to confirm this, and her suspicions of Joe.

Swiftly she slipped out into the corridor and made her way towards the head of the stairs. Here she would at least be able to note the direction from which the Fat Boy appeared.

So certain was she that her hypothesis would be confirmed that she almost missed him. Only her unusually wide and sensitive peripheral vision prevented her from doing so, for as she passed a short cul-de-sac passageway between two of the guest rooms, she caught a movement of the handle of the linen-cupboard door which stood at the end. Something too slow, careful, deliberately quiet about it made her hesitate.

'Joe!' called Wardle from below as Arabella pressed herself into the deep recess of a bedroom door.

Footsteps padded up the passageway and turned right, away from her place of concealment, towards the stair-head. Carefully she peered out, just in time to see the unmistakable shape of the Fat Boy move slowly down the stairs.

The linen cupboard was, forecastably, full of linen. It was more of a room than a cupboard and Arabella moved easily between the rows of shelves, breathing in the warm, friendly smell of newly pressed sheets. All kinds of memories of her childhood were brought back, not all of them happy. But all were quickly dismissed. Nostalgia and regret alike were little regarded in her scheme of things.

The question was, where had the Fat Boy come from? As there was no window, it had to be from above. The outline of a toe-print on top of a pile of sheets gave the clue, and seconds later Arabella was pulling herself up through a well-oiled trap into the attic storey of the house.

It was dark up here and she sat quietly for a few moments to let her eyes become accustomed to the gloom. It would have been wiser, she decided, to have changed out of her dressing gown into something more suitable for this kind of exploration; but if she had wasted time changing, this kind of exploration would not have been taking place.

Shapes, outlines at first but gradually hardening into forms, were beginning to emerge from the darkness. Lines of oak beams stretched away in all directions, solid, reliable, well able to take much more than a man's weight. Nevertheless someone had built athwart them a narrow cat-walk with a rail on one side. What was more, it was carpeted in some soft plastic material so that there was no chance of a carelessly placed foot causing a noise.

Arabella closed her eyes and tried to work out where her own bedroom was in relation to her present position. It wasn't easy, but at least she felt sure she had the direction right. Carefully she began to make her way along the walk.

When she reached the area which she believed to be above her room, she dropped down on all fours and began scanning the spaces between the beams for evidence of the suspected peephole. It was wood, not plaster, that she felt beneath her touch and she recalled the panelled ceiling of her bedroom. Doubtless this was common to all the house, but nevertheless she felt encouraged.

She found what she was looking for in the third interstice. Not a common or garden peephole but something more sophisticated. A narrow metal cylinder with a lens in it. Like a telescope. In fact, she found that it pulled out just like a telescope, and lying full length on the cat-walk she applied her eye to it.

She found herself looking at her bedroom door, which seemed an odd thing to look at. She jiggled the eyepiece between her fingers and her view changed rapidly from the bedroom door to the wall opposite. Fascinated she experimented and discovered that the instrument gave her a field of one hundred and eighty degrees clear vision up to about seven feet off the floor.

Clearly what was set into her ceiling was not a simple spy-hole but a complex optic lens working through refracted light. The picture given was tremendous in its clarity and a certain amount of magnification was attainable by turning the eye-tube like a normal telescope. She remembered how she had lain almost naked on the bed and shuddered to think of the Fat Boy gloating over his close-ups.

But next moment all thoughts of Joe were swept from her mind. Below, the bathroom door opened and two people emerged from it. She recognised them instantly. It was the Burtons, the Yorkshire couple she had met at lunch.

But why the hell are they searching my room? she asked herself. And (even more incredulously) what are they doing now?

For Mrs. Burton had slipped off the kimono-type robe she was wearing and Mr. Burton was attempting to establish a hand-hold on the ample bosom thus revealed. He was repulsed, but affectionately, as the truth dawned on Arabella.

It wasn't *her* room she was looking down into. There was no sign of her dress hanging outside the wardrobe, or of any of her gear on the dressing table. It was the odd viewpoint which had deceived. This was obviously the Burtons' own room.

Below, Mrs. Burton's resistance was clearly being eroded by constant pressure. Suddenly aware of the awful temptations of this kind of vantage point, Arabella took her eye away from the viewer. She could almost feel sympathetic towards Fat Joe! Almost.

She tried to reset the instrument exactly as she had found it, then began to crawl back along the cat-walk, confirming her suspicions as she did so. Every room below had one of these ingenius spy-viewers fitted. Such expenditure of effort and money obviously meant there was more than just a Peeping Tom's pleasure at stake. Sexual enthusiasm was one thing. This was much more sinister.

When she reached the linen-cupboard trap she hesitated. It would be pleasant to return to the normality of life below, if an attempt to turn the clock back a century and a half could be called normal. On the other hand the cat-walk stretched invitingly, or rather challengingly, ahead. The linen-cupboard was not its starting point, she was sure. It lay somewhere before her in the direction of the private part of the house.

In for a penny! she told herself and, standing up, began to stride with steady determination along the cat-walk.

It was almost disappointingly easy. The walk ended at a door which opened on to a narrow flight of stairs. Cautiously she descended and opened the single door which faced her.

She was in a corridor, but quite unlike the old corridors which wound their way around the Dickensian sector of the house. This one was lit by strip lighting and carpeted with the same yielding material that had muffled her steps along the cat-walk. It was the kind of corridor you might find in any modern office block. Rather too functional for even a modern hotel.

Several doors opened off it. Instinctively she kept on course for the one at the end. The door swung open silently at a touch and she entered.

The room she found herself in was large without being grand. A fire was dying in the pleasant old-fashioned fireplace. In the middle of the room was a solid rectangular table, set with blotters, freshly sharpened pencils, glasses and water jugs. She had seen this kind of table a hundred times before during her time with Cerberus Chemicals, had helped to get it ready. A board-room meeting; top-level business conference; anything of that ilk.

Somewhere there should be an agenda. Somewhere. But where? Even the waste-paper bins were empty. The grate, she noted, contained a lot of blackened paper ash. The fire was obviously there to provide more than just heat.

Swiftly she checked the blotters. All clean. Not so much as a single-pressure indentation visible. Whoever tidied up after this lot did a first-rate job. There was nothing here to tell what was going on.

With a sigh, she turned to the door through which she had entered. It would have to be one of the other rooms then.

Distantly she heard a door open and stopped in mid-stride. Someone was coming, but from what direction it was hard to say. Her ears were not as ultra-sensitive as her eyes. She retreated to the table and considered the room's three doors. One she knew about, but the others might lead anywhere. A store cupboard, perhaps, or a room full of gamekeepers with twelve-bores. She had been mad to venture this far. And in a dressing gown!

It was the door she had come in through! She was quite certain, not because of any noise outside but because of that highly refined intuition which had told her she was being watched. For a moment she thought, absurdly, of crawling under the table, but even as the thought formed she had moved across the room to the first of the other doors.

A store cupboard! Shelves packed with stationery. She caught a badly stacked pile of paper as it slid slowly out against her breast. Quickly she pushed the paper back. Another two strides took her to the other door. As she reached it, she heard a noise and turning saw the store-cupboard door, not properly shut, swing quietly open and the volatile stack of paper topple slowly out.

It was too late to do anything about it. They might think it was an accident. But at the moment flight was the only answer! She stepped through the second door and closed it behind her.

She was in an ante-room, boasting a small cocktail bar and an electric hot-plate. Clearly refreshments for those meeting next door were served from here. But there was no time for refreshment now. Someone was in the conference room behind her.

The next door took her into a corridor, not the modern-office type as before, but a continuation of the Dingley Dell style. The door at the far end about sixty feet away was, she was convinced, the door marked *Private* which had ended her exploration of the first floor. Almost sobbing with relief she sprinted down to it, regardless of the slapping of her slippers on the polished wood floor.

The door was heavily bolted. It took precious seconds to slide back the solid bolts. She turned the handle.

It was locked.

Behind her a door opened. Instinctively she pressed herself into the nearest doorway, fumbling for the handle behind her back. She found it, turned it, and stepped backwards into a darkened room.

No time for sight adjustment now. She closed the door quietly and stood in pitch-blackness, trying to hear noises outside through her own gasping breaths.

Nothing.

No. Something. Doors being opened and shut. She stepped back, frightened, bumping up against something which startled her. Turning, she explored it by touch.

Just a table. A plain wooden table by the feel of it. With something on it. Something cold. A piece of statuary? Her mind was exploring faster than her fingers and had reached its conclusions a moment before the door swung open behind her and dropped a rectangle of light over the thing on the table.

It was the small dark man who had been wheeled down from the hillside during lunch. He did not look reposeful in death.

'Looking for something, Miss Allen?'

She turned. In the doorway, his face twisted into an expression of mock deference, was the Fat Boy.

He looked potentially even less reposeful than the corpse behind her.

6

*I really cannot allow this matter to go any
further without some explanation.*

MR. SAMUEL PICKWICK

'Thanks,' said Arabella, meaning it, as she took the large
Scotch-and-soda Boswell had poured for her.

Boswell smiled pleasantly at the girl before him, looking
defenceless in her dressing gown which, pulled tightly around
her, merely managed to accentuate her excellent design. The
eyes which met his gaze over the rim of the heavy crystal
glass did not quite fit in with this picture of defencelessness.

He groaned inwardly. She was without doubt a problem. But
what kind of problem he had as yet no idea. And how to solve
it was even more remote from his mind.

'Right, Joe,' he said to the Fat Boy who stood expression-
lessly by the little cocktail bar. 'I'll deal with this.'

Joe did not move; his little beady eyes, sunk deep in the
fleshy face, flickered from the man to the woman. Then he
nodded, quite a feat for someone almost without neck.

'You're the boss,' he said, and left.

'So you're the boss,' said Arabella. 'What of?'

Boswell laughed.

'A figure of speech,' he said.

'A pretty gross figure,' she said, nodding at the door Joe had left through. 'Are you that blubber's boss?'

'He can't help being fat!' protested Boswell.

'No. He can help wanting to spread his fatness over me,' said Arabella.

'Good Lord! You're not going to turn out to be one of those neurotic women who think every man wants to rape them!'

Arabella shrugged, untouched by the gibe.

'I suspect he'd have had me on the table alongside that poor dead man. But that's just conjecture. I know he's been getting an eyeful of my feminine charms ever since I arrived here.'

'A cat can look at a queen.'

'Through a hole? In the ceiling? While the queen's getting dressed?'

Boswell poured himself a Scotch.

'Oh dear,' he said. 'I'm sorry about that. How did you notice?'

'I just got the feeling and put two and two together.'

'Interesting,' he said, looking at her closely. 'A good technique for survival.'

'Whose survival are we talking about, Mr. Boswell?'

'Call me Boz,' he said with a laugh. 'And I'll call you . . .'

'Miss Allen, till we sort this lot out. Well?'

'Well what?'

'I'd like an explanation.'

'Technically,' he said thoughtfully, 'You have been trespassing, you realise that? With burglarious intent too. You went through the cupboard next door, didn't you?'

'Minor offences,' said the girl, 'compared with invasion of privacy, intimidation and not reporting a murder.'

Boswell looked at her with sudden decision.

'Perhaps I'd better explain.'

'It would be appreciated.'

He settled himself comfortably in his chair and began.

'You've probably guessed that for some of the guests here this is more than just a Christmas holiday. And the number

55

of guests from abroad isn't just caused by an international love of Dickens.'

'You amaze me,' she murmured. He ignored her.

'What's going on here is in the nature of a business conference, one which involves a number of top industrial and commercial interests throughout Europe. There are proposals under consideration for the setting up of a huge international consortium which would have far-reaching effects throughout Western Europe.'

'What are they going to do? Level the Alps?'

Boswell looked serious.

'I'm not at liberty to tell you the nature of the enterprise. But it is large, many billions of pounds could be involved, and naturally any venture as grand as this has political overtones too. It could be a major factor in shaping our futures!'

'So you meet for a Dickensian Christmas!'

'Why not?' said Boswell. 'At this stage, secrecy is essential. When you worked for Cerberus Chemicals you must have known how much damage premature leakage of information could do to even a relatively small project.'

'How do you know I worked for Cerberus?' asked Arabella softly.

Boswell looked at her sheepishly.

'I'm sorry,' he said. 'We had to do a bit of background checking on the genuine guests. Just to make sure they were genuine, you understand. There are fortunes to be made by those who know the right answers at the right time. And some concerns are not much concerned about the way they get their information.'

'And the spy-holes?'

'Purely an easy means of checking from time to time that no one is in a room where they shouldn't be. They were certainly not intended as a source of pleasure for Peeping Toms. I'll see that Joe is severely disciplined.'

'What are you going to do? Cut off his jam-butties?' said Arabella, unsmiling. 'There is just one other thing. The dead man. What about him?'

'An accident, a terrible accident,' said Boswell. 'You were right, of course, it was a shotgun that did it. One of our 'keepers. With a 410, not a twelve-bore as you so keenly observed. But something like that is bad enough at the best of times—police swarming about, asking questions. In view of what's going on here at the moment, it could be disastrous. The police are trained observers. But, alas, they are not above temptation themselves, and there's a great deal of that around at Dingley Dell at the moment. So two days, that's all. Two days and it'll be reported. That's reasonable enough, isn't it?'

'That's not for me to say,' said Arabella, rising. 'Thank you for your explanation. Now I think I'd like to go and get dressed for the ball.'

Boswell remained in his seat and looked at her steadily.

'I hope we can rely on your complete discretion in this matter, Miss Allen.'

She returned his gaze unblinkingly.

'You'll just have to hope, Mr. Boswell. You've no alternative other than locking me up somewhere. In which case, I assure you, I'd scream, shout, fight, break windows, set things alight, anything till somebody took notice. As you said, *some* of the guests here are real holidaymakers, not financial wizards trying to conjure up a fast buck. They'd be interested in what happened to me. And on my release I'd sue you and those you represent for so much in damages that it would make the whole mysterious bloody enterprise financially non-viable to start with. Now, how do I get out of here? Via the attic and linen cupboard?'

Boswell rose, his arms held high in mock surrender.

'Peace, peace,' he said. 'No, I think you will find it less trying to keep to the flat this time. Joe!'

The door opened instantly and Joe appeared from the corridor.

'Unlock the door and let Miss Allen through, will you, And Joe. I'd like a word with you afterwards. Goodbye, Miss Allen. I look forward to seeing you at the ball.'

He watched her down the corridor till the big door had been locked and bolted behind her. Then he turned back to the bar, poured two drinks and went through into the conference room.

'Two questions,' said Wardle from his seat at the head of the conference table. He sipped the drink Boswell gave him and pulled a face. 'Irish. I drink Irish. Not this muck.'

'Two questions?' said Boswell.

'One. Is she what she seems, an innocent rich girl on holiday? And two. If she is, did she swallow your story?'

'I don't know,' said Boswell.

'Which?'

'Either. But there's a third question, isn't there? What do we do if she's *not* just an innocent rich girl and she *didn't* swallow my story?'

Wardle finished his drink with a grimace and moved to the door where he paused and looked back at Boswell.

'That's not a question,' he said. 'You don't need to make it a question when we both know there's only one answer.'

He went through into the other room and shortly there was a rattle of bottles.

'Now where's the Irish?' he called. '*That's* a real question."

But Boswell, his face clouded with thought, was no longer listening.

7

*The ball nights in Ba-ath are moments snatched
from Paradise; rendered bewitching by music,
beauty, elegance, fashion, etiquette and—and—
above all, by the absence of tradespeople . . .*

MR. ANGELO CYRUS BANTAM

By the time Arabella had returned to her room, sat in deep
contemplation for a while, stood on a chair precariously
placed on the bed to stick a piece of Elastoplast over the knot-
cum-peephole, got dressed and descended to the hall below,
the ball was under way.

There was to be dancing in the modern as well as the Victorian idiom, but the 'group' booked for the evening had been
delayed and the resident 'peasantry' were keeping things going
with three fiddles and a harp. Everyone seemed to be enjoying
the set-dances tremendously and Wardle was sweating and
laughing in equal proportions as he hopped round giving instructions and advice. The inevitable punch was being dis-
pensed at one end of the hall, though more sophisticated drinks
were available on request, and in an adjoining room a buffet
supper of immense proportions, from oysters to superbly
glazed beef-steak pies, was available.

Everyone wore period costume, with varying degrees of

success. It was a question of style. It had doubtless been half-humorously intended that Himmelstor had been given a general's uniform of the time of Waterloo, but his huge frame filled it so powerfully and convincingly that the effect was anything but comic. Likewise, the feathered turban which bowed and fluttered on Suzie Leclerc's head would have rendered a lesser woman absurd. Suzie made it look superb.

'Dance?' said Boswell, who must have come in behind her.

'No thanks. I'll just watch till I pick up the rules.'

He walked slowly round her, critically eyeing her dress. It was a high-waisted white satin gown, low cut at the front.

'Well?' she said.

'It's very beautiful,' he said, 'but I do need to get my own back. This very high waist had gone out by 1825 and I think you've probably got a couple of inches excess exposure at the top.'

She shrugged.

'You're talking of *Lunnun* fashion. Us poor country mice are always half a decade behind the metropolitans.'

'A good answer. It deserves some punch.'

His good intention was prevented by a noise outside in the entrance hall.

'Excuse me,' he said.

Through the open door Arabella saw five young men, carrying guitar cases and drums. Obviously the 'group' had arrived. What surprised her were the flakes of snow on their hair and shoulders.

'Sorry we're late, friend,' she heard one say to Boswell. 'Lucky to get here at all. It's bad to the north. You're just beginning to catch it.'

'Well, get your gear set up, then have a warm through and a drink before you start. We're doing nicely.'

'Thanks, mate.'

They removed their chunky fur coats and began lugging their equipment into the ballroom.

'Excuse me, lady,' said their spokesman, a dark serious-looking young man, to Arabella as he pushed by with a guitar-case. 'Thanks. Peace.'

'Peace to you too,' replied Arabella.

'I hope it gells,' said Boswell. 'This and this.'

He indicated the group and the three fiddles and the harpist.

'Why not? What's that they call themselves?'

She was looking at the bass drum which bore the letters T.T. and T.T.H.M.

'You'll never believe this,' said Boswell. 'It stands for *Thomas Traherne and The Temple-Haunting Martlet.*'

'I don't believe it. I've heard of them, but I still don't believe it.'

They laughed together. Boswell was encouraged.

'I'm sorry about before. I hope you'll be able to enjoy your holiday in peace now. I talked to Joe and I've had your peep-hole sealed off.'

'Me too,' she answered. 'As a matter of interest, just which of your guests *are* here for the consortium meeting?'

'I really mustn't say,' he murmured. 'Business ethics.'

'All right. Then what about this—how does it come about that a Victorian scholar is mixed up with big business?'

He spread his hands and shrugged grotesquely.

'A man's gotta live. And if you understand the Victorians you understand big business. But that's work. Tonight even big business rests. It's Christmas Eve. What about some good-will towards men in general and me in particular?'

She contemplated him calmly. The fiddles screeched to an ambitious finale. The dancers clapped. Then, almost without interval, another noise took over, cacophonous, violent, yet strangely familiar.

T.T. and T.T.H.M. hadn't bothered to wait for their warming drink but had launched straight into their first number.

'What *is* it?' cried Boswell.

'Don't you recognise it?' laughed Arabella, her feet tapping. 'It's *God Rest Ye Merry Gentlemen*, seventies style. Come on; these rules I already know.'

So saying, she pulled him on to the dance floor and began shaking herself at him in what he regarded as a most provocative fashion. After a moment he began shaking himself back and within seconds everyone in the room had taken to the floor and, in styles ranging from the apologetically self-conscious to the totally abandoned, the dance was on.

By midnight the international make-up of the party had clearly established itself. Songs and carols in most European languages could be heard from various corners of the ball-room. The wassail-bowl had been frequently replenished with brews of ever-increasing strength. Wardle, Boswell thought, must have decided that the danger of tongues being loosened by intemperance could best be countered by accelerating insensibility. The thought made him chuckle and the chuckle made him realise just how deeply he himself had dipped into the bowl.

He looked around the room. After their first dance Arabella had made it quite plain she had no intention of letting him monopolise her all evening. It might have been this which had set him off so energetically in search of his own good time. Pique was not an emotion becoming a scholar and a gentleman, he admonished himself. Where the hell was she? As long as she wasn't dancing with Robert E. Lee Sawyer again . . . No. There she was, chatting seriously to Mrs. Hislop. Good. Though why so serious? Mrs. Hislop had nothing to be serious about. Old man Bloodworth had evidently taken to his bed once more; he claimed he wasn't well enough to face this kind of activity.

Sawyer was at the far end of the room, his arm round Herr Bear, singing with him something which at this distance might have been *Heilige Nacht* or the *Horst-Wessel Lied*. The look of rapt devotion on Himmelstor's face gave nothing away. Leclerc leaned on the mantelshelf behind them, the shadow of a sneer on his finely featured face. It was odd that he should have taken up a position so near the band, which incidentally now deserved the title numerically at least, as T.T. and T.T.H.M. had been joined by the three fiddlers and the harpist. Thomas Traherne and his men were living up to their reputations as excellent musicians. Boswell, who had once had pretensions in that field himself, particularly admired the bass guitarist. Wardle had been responsible for the choice of the group, who were firm favourites in the top London party and reception set. He must remember to congratulate the fat man.

The fiddlers and the harpist did little but add extra decibels to the music's volume. Suzie Leclerc and Stephen Swinburne seemed to thrive on it. They had been dancing uninterruptedly in front of the musicians for the past hour. Boswell wondered what she was up to. She wasn't old enough, surely, to need the reassurance of the interest of youth? He tried to cut in once, but was firmly repulsed by the Frenchwoman whose body seemed to be straining to burst out of her dress.

Boswell realised he was letting his imagination show and turned toward the door, bumping into Wardle, who was standing on the threshold. He was wearing a magnificent ankle-length overcoat, dark purple, with three fur-trimmed shoulder-capes. Boswell reckoned it owed more to Carnaby Street than Dickens, but coveted it greatly all the same.

'Everything all right?' said Wardle.

'Fine. A bit warm though. I thought I'd take a turn outside.'

'I just looked. There's a full blizzard blowing up. There's a good foot of snow already in places and it looks set for ever. So I popped back in to grab my coat and I'm off to do my rounds, though it hardly seems worth it. Perhaps you'd like to go?'

'You've just put me off,' laughed Boswell. 'Have a drink before you go to keep the cold out.'

'I'll get them,' said Wardle, turning to the refreshment table. 'You have one to cool you down. Marvellous stuff drink; good for anything. Cheers.'

They drank in silence for a moment. Boswell had a strange feeling there was something final about it.

'Well, I'm off,' said Wardle. 'Keep your eyes skinned, eh? Everything's been covered, I think, but we can't afford any slip-ups. It's our reputation in the eyes of Europe that's at stake.'

Boswell grinned as he recognised the precise, upper-class tone Wardle was taking off. With a genial beam at the nearest guests, the fat man left the room. As he passed through the doorway into the dimmer light outside, he seemed to lose some of his substance, to shrink visibly. Suddenly uneasy, Boswell opened his mouth to call him back.

But he was already gone.

Boswell shook his head impatiently. It's that damned drink, he told himself in annoyance. No more tonight. He had to keep his wits about him.

He turned back to the dancing.

Something was going on. The dancers scattered, the women shrieking, as out among them advanced a hesitant figure with his arms outstretched and his face swathed with a white scarf. It was Sawyer.

'Blind-man's-buff!' cried someone.

'Super!'

T.T. and T.T.H.M. with minimal cacophony switched from *Rudolf the Red-nosed Reindeer* to *Three Blind Mice*. Suzie and Stephen were the last to finish dancing. They stood still, watching as Sawyer approached, until with suspicious accuracy, his outstretched fingers brushed her magnificent bosom. She turned unhurriedly away and Sawyer too turned and probed his way towards the middle of the room.

Good clean fun, thought Boswell. He'd have a report on Sawyer by the morning. Till then he was as harmless playing the goat in a blindfold as he was anywhere.

Sawyer was close now. Boswell stepped back.

'Ouch!' said Arabella.

'I am sorry,' he began as she danced on one foot before him.

'You clumsy oaf!' she said, and pushed him so hard he staggered and almost fell. But a pair of arms gripped and held him—to help, he thought at first, but immediately they grappled tight about his waist and a great roar of laughter went up.

'What the hell!' said Boswell.

'I got me a grizzly bear!' yelled Sawyer, tearing off his blindfold. 'Aw, hell! I wanted a female! Still, you'll have to do. Turn around!'

Protest was useless. The scarf was bound rapidly, tightly, round his eyes. Something was pressed into his hand. A glass.

'Come on,' said Sawyer. 'Drink up. It's in the rules.'

The glass was forced up to his lips and he swallowed a large mouthful, half choking. Someone hit him hard between the shoulder-blades.

'OK?' asked Sawyer. 'That's my boy. Now round you go. Round and round. And round. And round.'

His shoulders were gripped and he was spun forcibly round. Round and round, faster and faster. He tried to stop, but the hands kept on spinning him. Despite the blindfold, he seemed to see a streak of light, contracting and expanding as he span. Voices sounded in his ear. Shouting, laughing. The music beat louder, more insistently.

Stop! he opened his mouth to shout. Stop! But before he could get it out, the spinning stopped. And the music stopped. And the light died.

And everything was still.

When he opened his eyes he wished he hadn't. He was lying on his back and looming over him, not more than a foot away, was a grotesquely bloated face. He closed his eyes again and pressed his head back into what felt like a pillow. This was reassuring or not, depending on what the thing above him proposed to do.

He opened his eyes once more. The face had moved back and as he became used to the light, he realised he had been right about the lack of beauty, but wrong (he hoped) about the menace.

It was Joe, standing at the bedside, a malicious grin on his face. He was in his own room, Boswell realised. His cravat had been loosened, his jacket and shoes removed, otherwise he was fully clothed. He glanced at his watch, swore and swung his feet off the bed. The shafts of pain this sent jagging through his head took him by surprise and he slumped forward, covering his eyes with his hands.

'Like an Alka-Seltzer?' asked Joe.

'What the hell are you doing here?' snarled Boswell.

'Offering you an Alka-Seltzer,' said Joe pertly. 'You must have got stuck into that punch!'

'Who brought me here?'

'Oh, you had quite a little following!' laughed Joe. 'Sawyer. The Allen girl. Young Swinburne. And the French bit, to name but a pair. Christ! you looked bad. I hope it won't spoil your Christmas dinner!'

'Where are they now?' asked Boswell, trying to speak quietly.

'Who?'

'All of them. Any of them. Anybody at all!'

He wasn't succeeding in speaking quietly. He gave up altogether.

'Where the hell are they?' he bellowed. 'It's half an hour since I passed out, since someone slipped me a quietener. Who's been watching the stairs since then?'

The pain his words caused him was matched only by the consternation they gave birth to in the Fat Boy.

'Me. I mean . . . I'm sorry. I thought . . . a quietener? I thought you were drunk! So . . .'

'So you thought if he's getting in on the party, why should you bother to do your job? You're supposed to be keeping a check on who goes where. You know what's at stake. Bloody hell!'

He had stood up and was immediately regretting it. But to sit down again would be fatal. He began pushing his feet into his shoes.

'That Alka-Seltzer. Were you joking?'

Eager to please now, Joe passed him a tumbler full of gently bubbling water which he downed in a single draught.

'Jacket,' he said. Valet-like, the Fat Boy helped him put it on.

'Right,' he said. 'You get downstairs, see who's not in the ballroom. Report back here.'

Glad to get out, Joe left swiftly. Boswell picked up his phone and dialled an internal number.

'Hello,' said a cautious voice.

'Johnson? Boswell here. Get everyone on alert, will you? Check security up there, and do a scan along the attic, see what's going on in the rooms.'

'Will do.'

Boswell replaced the receiver and went to the window. His room overlooked the front of the house. He felt like some fresh air and pushed the window open, letting in a flurry of snowflakes. As Wardle had forecast, the wind was rising and already it was difficult to see any distance through the oblique lines of snow. Straining his eyes, he could make out the barn and perhaps even the beginnings of the double colonnade of trees which marked the drive. Much more of this and they would be cut off.

The Fat Boy returned, looking worried. Following him through the door came a gust of distant music. Whatever else was happening, T.T. and T.T.H.M. were still going strong. Another thought came to Boswell as he heard them.

'Has anyone seen Mr. Wardle?'

'No. I mean, I haven't. And he's not around downstairs.'

'Blast!'

His former unease came back. Wardle should be back in the house by now. No one would stop outside in this weather longer than he had to. Unless he had to. He shook the thought from his head. Half an hour unconscious and he was assuming everything had gone haywire. Prima donna Boswell they would call him!

But better a prima donna than a red-nosed fool. The point where you stopped worrying about your own efficiency rating and alerted the outer security ring was far from being a fixed mark. To Boswell it came when he found himself thinking *if things get worse in the next hour, then I'll get in touch*. When that thought came he usually got in touch immediately.

'About downstairs,' began Joe.

'Hang on,' said Boswell, reaching for the telephone. Before he could pick it up, it rang. It was Johnson again.

'Everyone's alert,' he said. 'We checked around. One thing, the radio's on the blink.'

'Damn,' said Boswell. 'Can you fix it?'

'We're looking at it now. It could be bad,' Johnson said cautiously. 'We've checked the rooms. Nothing going on except that Miss Allen's observation point's been blocked off. And Mr. Bloodworth's too.'

So Arabella, quite rightly, hadn't accepted his reassurance that her peep-hole would no longer be used! But Bloodworth . . . why should the old man want to keep himself hidden? And how did he know?

He replaced the receiver and immediately dialled an outside number. It would be an open line. With the radio, it hadn't seemed necessary to fit a scrambler. Still, beggars couldn't be choosers.

A beggar's choice was even more limited, it seemed. Nothing was coming through the receiver. He jiggled the rest. Quite quite dead.

The lines must be down along the road. From the road to Dingley Dell itself they were laid underground so that no anachronistic telegraph poles should spoil the outward effect. The snow must be really heavy. Soon they could be absolutely cut off.

Quickly he dialled Johnson's number again.

'Radio?' he asked.

'Dead as a doornail.'

'Who's our best local man?'

'Colley, I'd say. He knows hereabouts like the back of his hand.

'Get him.'

He nodded at Joe who had been standing patiently by the door. The Fat Boy cleared his throat.

'Everyone's in the ballroom or accounted for, except these. Miss Allen, Madam Leclerc, young Mr. Swinburne. And Sawyer.'

Boswell swore.

'Pardon?' said Colley's voice in his ear.

'Not you. Listen, Colley, have you seen the snow outside? OK. Do you think you can get through it to the village?'

A pause.

'I think so, Mr. Boswell. If I went now.'

'You're sure?'

'Not sure. But there's places I could hole up at on the way if I got stuck. The old gate-cottage for instance. And Adam's Farm up along Two-Lane Hill.'

'Fair enough. I don't want you getting yourself frozen to death. When you reach a phone that's working, ring this number and ask for the Major. No message, just answer questions, that'll be enough. Here's the number.'

Twice he recited it, then replaced the receiver, feeling relieved. Colley would get through if anyone could. Though probably he was being an old woman in any case.

Joe was still waiting.

'You not gone yet?' said Boswell rudely.

'Gone where?'

'Find those people. Get everybody on to it. I want them located.'

'Do you want them taken?' asked Joe hopefully.

'Taken? Taken? You mean, "Hands up. Quick march!" Don't be a bloody fool. Just find them and watch them, that's all. And Mr. Wardle too. See if you can get hold of him.'

Joe left and Boswell followed soon after. His first stop was Arabella's room. There was no reply to his knock and he opened the door. The room was empty. Swiftly he moved on. As he passed the linen-cupboard alcove he heard a noise and stopped. For a moment he wondered if Arabella or someone else was trying to repeat her feat of climbing into the attic *via* the trapdoor. She would be disappointed. It had been securely screwed down earlier in the evening. But a few seconds listening at the door convinced him that someone had found a much more personal use for the warm, clean-smelling darkness within. A man's voice and a woman's voice, too low to be distinguishable, but the activity they were engaged in was unmistakable.

Boswell passed on, knowing he should have interrupted them. Wardle would have done, but Wardle had been in the business much longer than he had. In fact this was probably his swan-song. Soon the stout man would be entering on a well-earned retirement. Boswell wished to God he would turn up quickly and safely.

Next stop was Bloodworth's room. He knocked.

'Come in,' quavered the old man's voice.

Boswell entered. Bloodworth was in bed, reading a book. He did not look well, but his eyes were bright.

'Just checking to see you've got all you need, sir,' said Boswell. 'Would you like anything sent up?'

'No, thank you. Just stop that blasted noise downstairs, that's all I ask.'

'It won't be too long now,' smiled Boswell, opening the

bathroom door. 'Soap, towels. You seem to have everything. Good night then.'

He left and went on towards the sealed-off conference area but was intercepted near the stair-head by the Fat Boy.

'Anything?' he asked.

'Not a sign,' answered Joe. 'Mr. Wardle must have come back though. There's a set of waterproofs hanging up to dry in the back kitchen.'

Boswell's heart jerked.

'Waterproofs?' he said, remembering Wardle immersing himself in the long, multi-caped Victorian greatcoat.

'Show me.'

The wet waterproofs hung neatly among four or five others on a row of hooks along the wall of the small alcove which led from the back kitchen to the outside door. Some of the snow had not yet melted and a steady trickle of water-drops splashed to the tiles below. Something of the shape of their last wearer still remained to give the black oilskins an air of menace, as if they might have climbed down from the peg themselves and gone out into the night.

Boswell opened the door and once again looked out into the blizzard. There was a sill of snow three feet deep against the door and deeper still along the outside wall. The main strength of the wind which was gusting to gale force was being hurled from the east obliquely against the rear of the house, otherwise the drifts would have been much deeper. He dreaded to think what they must be like against the eastern side-wall. He hoped to God Colley would have the sense to turn back if necessary.

'Come on,' said Boswell suddenly.

'What? Into *that*?'

'Come on, I said,' snapped Boswell, pulling on a waterproof top.

'Hello. What's going on?' said another voice from the shadows at the end of the large kitchen.

Out into the pool of light shed by the solitary bulb which lit the alcove stepped Arabella.

'Something wrong?' she asked.

'Maybe,' said Boswell, uncertain how to deal with this

70

development. His training told him to stop and question her but his instincts were driving him out into the blizzard. At least it seemed unlikely that she had been the woman in the linen room.

'It's Wardle,' he said finally.

'Mr. Wardle?' she said uncomprehending. 'You don't mean you think he's out in *that*?'

'Could be.'

'I'll come with you,' she said.

Before he could answer she seized the freshly used water-proofs from their peg, pulled the cape over her head, and began clambering into the rubber boots.

'You'll ruin your dress,' was all Boswell could find to say.

'No,' she said, and with a dismissive glance at Joe she pulled her skirts up above her knees, bent forward to pull her short train through between her legs and fastened it with a brooch-pin at her midriff.

She did it expertly. As if she had done it before, thought Boswell. Was he mistaken, but did her face look rather chapped as though it had been offered to the elements recently? Her hair did not quite fit into the souwester hat she pulled on. Were the stray tresses damp? But before he could test his theory she had stepped out into the storm and invalidated any evidence there might have been that she had been out before. Which was nice and handy too.

'Come on, Joe,' said Boswell, and followed Arabella.

'Which way?' she screamed.

It was a good question. Shading his face from the wind and snow, he studied the ground. Any tracks there might have been would have been covered up in a matter of seconds. Except perhaps out ahead in the relative shelter of the grove of elms which stood between the house and the Jockey Pond.

Head down he plunged forward towards the trees and moved his flashlight slowly over the snow, still thick here despite the vault of protective branches overhead.

'What are we looking for?' shouted Arabella, clinging to his arm. Behind her, looking as miserable as the Ancient Mariner, stood the Fat Boy, obviously feeling the bitter cold even through his very generous layers of protective fat.

'Tracks,' said Boswell. 'Though bloody Tonto and the Lone Ranger would be hard pushed to find anything in these conditions.'

The snow did look as if it might have been disturbed here, but by what and when was beyond his powers of interpretation. He moved forward hopelessly. Then in the yellow ring of torchlight he saw a beautifully delineated boot-print. It was alongside a huge-boled elm, to the leeward, which explained why it had not yet been filled in. It was pointing towards the house.

Boswell looked out into the shifting whiteness of the snow-storm, straining his eyes in vain for a sight of movement.

'Wardle!' he shouted. 'Wardle!'

But the wind slipped between his mouth and the words and span them off sideways into the night.

'It's no good!' shouted Joe, clearly eager to get back.

He was probably right. But Boswell was deeply concerned now. If Wardle was out here somewhere, and in need of help, any delay would certainly be fatal. No one could survive this stuff for long, especially someone unable to move.

He ignored Joe, brushed off the silent girl and moved forward again. Only a faint hollow in the snow told him he had reached the pond. He hesitated here, eyes straining again. Ahead he thought he could see something dark against the whiteness of the snow. The flakes eddied and whirled. The dark patch faded, then reappeared.

Reluctant though he was to risk the strength of the ice, he knew he had to go forward. It might be Wardle lying there.

'What are you doing?' called Arabella, as he began to move forward. 'Don't be so stupid!'

He ignored her and took another step. Through the cushion of snow he felt the ice, hard and solid. With growing confidence he trod another couple of steps.

Behind him and to the side, wisely keeping a couple of yards away, came Arabella. Even more wisely, Joe kept his bulk shivering on the bank.

The mystery of the dark shape was solved when Boswell got within a couple of yards of it. It was quite simply not a solid

72

shape at all, but a hole. The hole in the ice which Frau Cow had sunk by her accident that afternoon.

At the same time disappointed and relieved, Boswell turned to go, becoming aware for the first time that Arabella had accompanied him.

'Let's go!' he yelled angrily. 'We don't want another accident.'

She held her ground, staring at the hole, and said something.

'What?' he shouted impatiently.

'Shouldn't it have frozen again?'

This time he caught the words, but it took a second or two for their significance to sink in. Then he turned back to look at the hole.

It was true. With the sub-zero temperatures they had had all day it was almost certain that a new skin of ice would have rapidly reformed on the surface of Frau Cow's hole. Only a thin skin, perhaps, but certainly strong enough in a few hours to bear the weight of the snow.

In which case, there shouldn't be a hole visible at all.

He began to move forward again. Beneath his weight as he neared the hole, the ice began to groan and protest.

'Careful!' shouted Arabella.

He glanced at her and for a second forgot Wardle in his fear that she had plunged down through the ice. Then he realised that she had dropped on all fours, spreading her weight around as she moved forward. It seemed like a good idea and he did the same.

Two feet from the hole, he halted and shone the torch into the water. Nothing. But quite clearly the new ice-skin had formed and had once again been shattered. He felt sick with worry.

Then beside him the girl screamed. There was no panic in the scream, no hysteria. Just an outcry of shock, horror, quickly bitten off.

He moved towards her.

'What is it?' he called, 'Are you all right?'

She didn't answer but knelt there staring down at the ice. He shone his torch where she was looking. Her hands had brushed away the snow as she crawled forward and for a moment he could see nothing as the yellow light reflected back from the polished surface. Then, like a vision in a crystal ball, it formed tremulously to his sight.

'Oh Christ!' he said.

Dimly visible through the flawed and semi-opaque ice, staring sightlessly upwards at the world of air and sky he had left forever, was a man's face.

It was hideously distorted, unrecognisable without further clues. But even as they watched, some deep current in the water caught at the body and it slid out of sight, moving down obliquely so that the whole body slid past the clear patch. Three fur-trimmed capes on a long warm coat, Boswell counted.

Then it was gone, and the snow was already covering the window in the ice.

8

*There was just such a wind, and just such a fall
of snow, a good many years back, I recollect . . .
It was Christmas Eve too, and I remember on
that very night he told us the story about the
goblins that carried away old Gabriel Grub.*

THE OLD LADY

Arabella wasn't the swooning kind, but her legs felt so weak
and nerveless that it was only with a considerable effort of
will and much help from Boswell that she made it back to the
bank. It was not a labour of love on his part. She could sense
his straining impatience under his stiff waterproofs. The
moment he was sure she was off the treacherous ice he released
her and yelled for Joe. The Easter-egg shape of the Fat Boy
came rolling through the unceasing lines of snow.

'Wardle's dead,' grunted Boswell.

'He may not be!' protested Arabella. 'Shouldn't we try
to . . .'

'He's dead,' snarled Boswell. 'Joe, get Miss Allen back to
the house. We've got trouble, so make it quick. I'll be in the
radio room. That bloody thing's got to work. You cover the
back of the house, I'll send round one of the others to cover
the front. If anyone's stupid enough to try to leave on a night
like this, stop them.'

'Won't they be gone now?' queried Joe.

'Whoever it was didn't just come here to kill Wardle,' said Boswell. 'Quick as you can.'

Without even a glance at Arabella, he turned and ran off towards the house.

'Come on,' grunted Joe, jerking the girl to her feet. His touch completed the process of recovery through indignation which Boswell's callousness had started.

'I can manage!' she snapped, and set off bravely through the snow.

Back in the warm kitchen of Dingley Dell she divested herself of her snow-caked waterproofs.

'You all right?' asked Joe, and hardly waited for her distant nod before disappearing into the night once more. Immediately she felt boorish and stupid. Boorish because he had only helped her, after all, and stupid because there were questions she needed answers to.

She ran down the short passageway and flung open the door. He had only gone a few steps and was still visible among the whirling flakes. At the noise of the door, he turned and stepped back towards her. In his hand, black and menacing, was an automatic pistol.

She stared at him for a moment, then gently closed the door and went back into the kitchen.

Surprisingly her ball-dress had suffered very little from being kilted and crushed beneath the oilskins. She recovered her reticule from the kitchen table, combed her hair (which had not been quite so resilient) and decided that the first thing she really needed was a stiff drink. The distant music sounded as gaily as ever. Clearly news of Wardle's death had not yet reached the revellers. And clearly also, if the precedent of the groom's death was anything to go by, Boswell would do his best to keep it from them. Just where she herself stood in these mists and twists of intrigue she had not yet decided. But if the wassail was still flowing she surely deserved some of it to flow her way.

The party seemed as merry as ever. The fiddles and harp had taken over again and Thomas Traherne and his ensemble were helping themselves to refreshments. Their bass guitarist, a long slim youth with bushy red hair and delicate, freckled features, passed Arabella a glass of punch with a courteous little bow.

'Thanks,' she said.

'You're welcome, lady,' he said. 'You look as if you've been out in the cold.'

My! she thought. Aren't you the sharp-eyed one!

'I put my head out of the door for a breath of air. But only for a second!' she lied. 'It's nasty.'

'Still bad, is it? I hope it clears by Boxing Day. We don't want to get stuck.'

'Well, certainly no one's getting away from here in the next few hours!' said Arabella.

The full implications of the thought struck her coldly. Whoever had pushed the dead (or unconscious) Wardle through the ice wouldn't be able, even if he wished, to head for the hills. The roads would be quite impassable and anyone on foot would find it hard to survive. The only place for him to go was back to the house. No wonder Boswell had been so keen to get back here as quickly as possible!

She finished her drink, smiled at the worried musicians and made for the door. She felt utterly at odds with all the merriment that was going on here. There was too much she didn't understand. And far too much that she suspected.

Her hand was grasped as she crossed the dance floor.

'You with me will dance? Yes?' boomed Herr Bear, damply red from drink and exertion.

'I with you will dance, no,' she answered pushing by. Frau Cow stared at her coldly from an isolated wallflower position. Near the door, she passed the elder Swinburnes having a polite, totally non-animated conversation with Jules Leclerc. They paused as she went by, and she felt their eyes on her as she left the room.

It was with relief that she found herself alone in the hallway once more, a relief that modified into unease as she mounted the stairs and the light and noise of the ball receded behind her. Her previous train of thought was picked up once more. Wardle's killer was in the house. It was very quiet and lonely up here. The pseudo-candelabra which lit the landing took authenticity to the point of dimness. She gathered up her skirts round her ankles and made for her room at the best speed she could. But she'd only gone a couple of yards when the sound of someone approaching brought her to a halt.

The thought went rapidly through her mind that tonight it was a good idea to see others first without being seen. Quietly she slipped sideways into the linen-cupboard alcove through which she had earlier gained access to the attic. Seconds later a figure swept rapidly by.

It was Suzie Leclerc.

And on her pale face was such an expression of panic and dismay that Arabella could see at once that not all the un-pleasantnesses of the evening had happened outside.

For a second Arabella hesitated between going after Suzie to see if she could help, and going in search of Boswell to seek his advice. Selfishly she decided that neither alternative was equal to getting back to her own room as quickly as possible, locking the door and sitting down to have a good, clear think.

But seconds later, as she stood clutching the door-jamb for support, her hand at her mouth in the classic gesture of near-vomitory shock, she knew she had been wrong. Anything was better than standing here looking down at the pathetically fragile body of Stephen Swinburne, whose candlewax pallor flamed into the startling crimson of the blood which had poured through his matted hair and stained the white pillow beneath his head.

I didn't shriek! she found herself thinking proudly. I didn't shriek. Or did I? Twice in a night, and this time I didn't shriek. I must be getting hardened.

The crazy whirl of thoughts did their work of cutting her off from the horrifying reality of the situation long enough for her rationality to regain control. Absurdly she found her-self completing the return to normality by bending down to pick up a sheaf of typewritten papers which lay scattered by the door and stuffing them into her bag. Keep Britain tidy, even when there was a dead boy in your room. A dead boy? She recalled her protests when she and Boswell had left Wardle. It seemed impossible that this pale figure could con-tain any life, but she quickly approached the bed and took the boy's hand. To her surprise and relief there was an easily perceptible pulse, not strong, but not desperately faint either. Steeling herself, she peered down at the boy's head. The initial impression that the top of his skull must have been crushed like an eggshell also turned out to be wrong. There had clearly been a substantial blow given and God knew what damage might have been done to the skull. But the wound itself was only two or three inches long. Only! she thought wryly. Still it was better than the gaping hole which at first had seemed necessary to let all this blood out.

Medical attention was now much more the priority than investigation of the crime. She seized the bedside phone and jiggled the rest impatiently.

'Yes?' said a man's voice. Cool. Impersonal.

'This is Arabella Allen,' she said rapidly. 'There's been an accident. No, an assault. The thing is, Mr. Swinburne's been injured. Seriously. He's in my room. Now can you get hold of a doctor . . . ?

But she tailed off, realising the phone had gone dead. She was still angrily trying to re-establish contact when she heard footsteps sprinting down the corridor and seconds later Boswell and two other men she recognised as the gamekeepers appeared in the doorway.

Boswell strode over to the bed and peered down at the wounded youth.

'Oh, *that* Swinburne,' he said.

'Does it matter which?' demanded Arabella furiously. 'What he needs is a doctor, not you and your gun-dogs.'

'It's being taken care of,' said Boswell, unaffected by her anger which subsided immediately as a new problem rose in her mind.

'How will he get here?' she asked. 'The blizzard . . .'

She crossed to the window, pulled back the curtain and peered out. The snow was still being whirled frenetically round the house by the shrieking wind. Boswell's hand took the curtain from her and covered the window once more. The gesture appeared casual but it did not feel so.

'You're right,' he said. 'No one will get through this. Fortunately one of the guests is a doctor.'

79

'One of *your* guests?' she asked sharply.

'No, actually,' he replied. 'It was a need we did not anticipate.'

'Like a great deal else,' retorted Arabella, but Boswell had turned away and was talking in a low voice to the gamekeepers. They turned to go, meeting in the doorway Alf, the coach-driver, who had with him Mrs. Hislop.

She went straight to Stephen and began her examination, moving with a precise efficiency which belied the impression she gave of the prototype middle-class suburban housewife.

'I have no equipment,' she said suddenly.

'Dingley Dell has a fairly well-stocked medical room,' said Boswell with easy charm. 'What do you need?'

'An X-ray machine for a start,' Dr. Hislop said coldly. 'I take it it's impossible to get him to a hospital in this weather.'

'I'm afraid so.'

'Then if we can't move him to hospital, I suggest it would be better not to move him at all. This isn't his room?'

She looked at the evidence of Arabella's occupation clearly to be seen.

'No. It's mine.'

'He'll have to stay here,' said the woman. 'Now quickly. Show me this allegedly well-equipped medical room.'

Twenty minutes later she proclaimed Stephen to be as comfortable as she could make him. He was still unconscious, but there was some colour in his cheeks; and now that his head wound was washed and dressed, and the gory pillow had been removed, he no longer looked like an escapee from hell. His parents had arrived in the room after the best part of the transformation had taken place and Boswell had ushered them away in the face of Dr. Hislop's clear disapproval. Arabella herself had unconsciously fallen into the role of nurse and her efforts at assistance had won a couple of approving grunts from the doctor.

'That's it,' said Mrs. Hislop finally, and went into the bathroom to wash her hands. When she came out she had almost visibly reverted to her housewife self.

'I'm afraid we've both ruined our dresses,' she said with a rueful smile. 'Thank God they belong to the hotel!'

'Mine doesn't,' said Arabella.

'No? That explains it! I've been admiring it all night and wishing they'd given it to me instead! Never mind. Get those blood-stains into cold water right away and you should be all right.'

There was a tap at the door and Boswell came in.

'OK? How's he going to be?'

'Hard to say till he recovers consciousness. We've done all we can with what we've got here. The surface wound's nothing. That'll heal. It's the possible skull fracture and, more importantly, any brain damage we've got to worry about.'

'We'll get him to hospital as soon as possible,' said Boswell. 'Meanwhile, Doctor, if you could say something reassuring to his parents it would be a kindness.'

'Perhaps. Perhaps not,' she said. 'I'll speak with them, of course.'

At the door she paused.

'By the way, Mr. Boswell. How did you know my profession? I deliberately keep quiet about it when I'm on holiday, otherwise I get everybody's ailments with my breakfast.'

Boswell shrugged.

'I'm not sure. Perhaps it was something your uncle said.'

She looked at him disbelievingly, then left. Arabella looked down at the young man on the bed. He seemed to be peacefully sleeping and she felt suddenly optimistic. He would be all right. She picked up the telephone.

'What do you want?' asked Boswell.

'Coffee,' she answered. 'And answers.'

'Answers? Later. There's things to be done.'

She ignored him. 'Hello?' she said into the phone. 'Miss Allen here. Mr. Boswell would like some coffee to be brought to my room. Quickly please. And two cups.'

She replaced the receiver and spoke to Boswell.

'I want to know what's going on,' she said. 'And this time, try to make it the truth.'

9

*I am delighted to hear it . . . I like to see sturdy
patriotism, on whatever side it is called forth.*

MR. SAMUEL PICKWICK

Boswell sat, bleary-eyed, at the end of Arabella's bed and felt
himself disadvantaged by the clear grey eyes which surveyed
him coolly through the steam of a coffee-cup.

He had not known such a bad start to a Christmas Day
since at the age of six, over-enthusiastic to see what presents
lay at the foot of the family Christmas tree, he had tripped
in the pre-dawn darkness and arrived at the bottom of the
stairs with a broken ankle. Now the memory filled him with
deep nostalgia.

'The truth?' he echoed.

'Yes,' the girl said firmly. 'Forget your commercial interests
and business consortium. Speak truth and shame the devil.'

The truth, he thought. He might as well, it made little difference. He hadn't made up his mind yet about Miss Arabella
Allen. She might well be in the business in which case there
was little he could tell her which she wouldn't know already.
Or she might be straight. In which case she'd be better off—
and safer—knowing. In any case, the wise move was to per-
suade her he accepted she was straight and the best way of
doing this was through the truth.

'It's been a hell of a night,' he said bitterly. 'And you want me to start Christmas with the truth? All right. What I'm going to tell you is restricted information. That means it's only known to the Prime Minister, security top brass, and evidently anyone in the northern hemisphere who cares to ask. For all I know it's been a popular topic of discussion today over iced plum-duff on Bondi Beach.'

He paused. Arabella smiled sweetly.

'Are you going to tell me or shall I wait till I read the Australian newspapers?'

'I'll tell you. Are you sitting comfortably? Then I'll begin. I wasn't being altogether untruthful when I told you yesterday that there was a European business consortium meeting here at Dingley Dell. The need for a rationalisation of European commercial energies has been long recognised. That's what the Common Market's all about. And as the modern state is essentially an economic unit, economic modifications must by definition lead to political modifications. You follow me? This was clearly recognised in the Treaty of Rome. Eventually it's quite clear we'll work our way to a United States of Europe situation, those of us who don't join the other United States, that is.'

'Boswell for president? Is that it?'

'Thank you but no. The point is this. Everything's in the melting pot, the heat's on, and I don't think it'll slacken off till we are all indissolubly joined. But the most difficult thing of all isn't economic or military or even strictly political. The hard core, the most heat-resistant bit of all, lying at the centre of every state, is security. When everything else is nice and liquid the little hard lumps still rattling around the bottom of the pot will be the national security agencies. If you let the mixture cool with those still in it, you might as well not bother.'

'Like a lumpy rice pudding?'

'Your domestic images don't impress me,' said Boswell. 'Anyway, feelers have been going out for some time about a merging of interests. Imagine what it would mean! If we could bring together all the expertise and information of all the Western European systems, we could make the CIA and KGB look like the Women's Institute!'

'Don't get carried away,' said Arabella, looking at him curiously. 'What's your stake in all this? You don't really want to be president after all, do you?'

'I'm sorry,' said Boswell sheepishly. 'No, I'm just an enthusiast. Not for security work itself, you understand. I've been at it too long. I was recruited while I was still at university.'

'You mean Dickens is a cover?' Arabella was incredulous.

'Hell, no. But being a well-known academic does give one plenty of opportunities for world-wide travel, so I've received every encouragement from my masters. But, as I was saying, it's the idea of a United Europe I'm enthusiastic about. And I don't see how it can be achieved without bringing together the national security forces. And that's what this is all about. Everything's still at such an early stage that any formal open meeting is out of the question. The very nature of our business makes it undesirable for these men to appear officially in public anyway.'

'These men being...?'

'Didn't I say?' asked Boswell. 'We've got the top men of nearly every security force in Western Europe gathered here. It seemed the best cover we could devise. A Christmas break with the family! The set-up here is quite legitimate. But it's been under our aegis since it started. So here they came from far and wide. A Dickensian Christmas. Peace and goodwill to all men.'

He spoke bitterly. Arabella felt an urge to comfort him, but when she spoke her voice was still neutral.

'Is it your fault that two men are dead?'

He was startled by the question.

'No!' he said, then more quietly; 'No. Wardle is—was—in charge of security on the ground while we are here. I'm just an educated office boy. Till now. Now I take over; there's no one else. Not while the blasted snow keeps falling.'

He drew back the curtains and peered out of the window.

'Don't you share responsibilities then?' she asked, irony just audible.

'Not in this game. You've enough of your own without sharing. But you do inherit them. The next one to be killed, that'll be my responsibility.'

It was her turn to be startled. She rose and joined him by the window.

'You expect more killings?'

'Sawyer's still loose. He doesn't seem to set himself any limits.'

'Sawyer? How do you know it's Sawyer?'

'Who else? No one else got in here who hadn't had our famous one hundred per cent security check which only misses out three or four times a week. I should have locked the bastard up the minute he appeared.'

'Have you done any checking on him?'

'Naturally, but nothing's through yet. Nor is likely to be till they get the phones working again.'

'But what about the radio?'

He laughed grimly at her.

'Didn't I tell you about the radio? I went straight up to the radio room when we got back inside. We thought the damn' thing had just gone on the blink. But closer examination proved us wrong. It's been beautifully, expertly, wrecked!'

The bedroom door opened and the Swinburnes peered in.

'Please come in,' said Boswell. 'I'm afraid he's still out.'

'Dr. Hislop told us,' whispered Mrs. Swinburne, 'but I would just like to sit for a while . . .'

'Of course. I'll send some more coffee.'

Taking Arabella firmly by the elbow, he led her to the door.

'Boswell!'

It was Swinburne.

'Yes, sir?'

'I'd like a word. Fifteen minutes? In the conference room then.'

Arabella raised her eyebrows questioningly at Boswell as he carefully closed the door.

'Swinburne? Is he . . . ?'

'Oh yes,' he said. 'He is. Our Man in Whitehall. Mother. Uncle. C. M. Z. You can make up your own code-name. He's the one who walks the corridors of power and when things

85

start going wrong for poor bastards in the field he presses the button that brings the lions streaming into the arena.'

'Poor Boswell,' said Arabella with real sympathy.

'At least I'm alive,' he said gloomily. 'Where are you going?'

'Back in there. I want my clothes for a start. And I'll want somewhere to sleep. Stephen's room, I suppose. You are still running an hotel here, aren't you? Good. So can you please arrange things?'

'Of course. By the way, for the record, I don't suppose you've got the faintest idea what that young man was doing in your bed in your bedroom?'

'Not the faintest! But that reminds me—the excitement put it quite out of my mind.'

Swiftly she told him about her encounter with Suzie Leclerc.

'Interesting,' he said. 'Any other snippets you've overlooked?'

For a moment he thought she was going to say something else, but she hesitated briefly and the moment was gone.

'Nothing,' she said.

'OK. See you later.'

Gloomily he made his way along the corridor towards the conference room, stopping only to confirm that Dave, the coach-guard, was in position to keep an eye on Arabella when she left the bedroom. It would be nice to trust her absolutely, but it was a luxury he couldn't afford. This was his first big operation and already it was a disaster. Even without the attack on young Stephen things had been bad. Old Swinburne had been desperately keen to put up a good show under the scrutiny of some of Europe's most highly critical security men. The two deaths would cause him acute professional discomfort, but this was nothing compared with the personal anger the attack on his son had produced.

He wasn't looking forward to the interview with him. Meanwhile there were other things to worry about. Sawyer was on the loose somewhere, almost certainly in the house. No one unequipped could survive outside for long on a night like this, and the nearest shelter was the village nearly ten miles away.

He seriously doubted whether even Colley could make it. Sawyer certainly couldn't.

The thought brought him some small satisfaction. If the killer was in the house there was no way of evading capture. Boswell had already started his men searching, a task aided by the fact that the party below showed no sign of breaking up. They were back on the country dancing again, fiddles and harp going like billy-oh! Only Arabella of those not actively involved in the conference suspected anything untoward was going on. Except poor Stephen. And the Hislop woman. Damn! One was too many. But at least if Sawyer could be found it might reassure the delegates that they could proceed in safety.

If he could be found in the next fifteen minutes it might even take the edge off Swinburne's wrath. He increased his pace, his jaw set with determination.

Sawyer watched him go through the crack of a barely opened door. He grinned widely. In his left hand was a half-eaten turkey leg, in his right a dull black automatic. He now slipped this into the scarlet cummerbund he wore round his waist and took both hands to the turkey.

'He's tougher than he looks, that cookie,' he grunted as he chewed.

'You're a fool, Tarantyev,' said the man behind him calmly. Sawyer laughed at the affront.

'This is the life, huh? Food, drink, and all the excitement you can manage!'

'You were supposed to be on the outside, observing,' said the other, ignoring him. 'That's all. Not drawing attention to yourself, then killing those sent to investigate. Not foolhardily pushing yourself into the house.'

'It was all set up,' protested Sawyer without heat.

'As a second line of attack if for any reason I did not make it,' answered the other. 'Then to kill Wardle! And the boy. We could have used the boy.'

'That's what them Frenchies thought too,' laughed Sawyer. 'You think there's anything to drink in here?'

'For Godsake! This was supposed to be a quiet operation.

We were here to observe, note and report. Unobtrusively. Undetected. I feared the worst when they told me Tarantyev was in charge of the operation. But this is worse even than I feared! I see now why you had to get out of America so quickly.'

'Where I had been for seven years,' said Sawyer, serious now. 'And where I had done more damage in seven than Lonsdale or Philby did here in twenty! Let me tell you something, sonny; the way I work, no one likes to give the go-ahead. They're all like you, a bunch of frigging filing clerks. But they like my results, oh yes. So they put me in charge. Remember that. You know my authority. You *don't* know the full picture of this operation. So just take orders. And do it *my* way.'

'Pah! Look at you! Like Douglas Fairbanks!'

'Yes, sir. And I always get the girl. Now you get back down below and make with the merriment. I've got things to do. You'll know when I need you. These fools think they're chasing me. What they don't know is, I'm chasing them!'

He laughed freely and uninhibitedly. The other man, his face wreathed with grave doubts, carefully opened the door and peered out.

'Good luck,' he said reluctantly: 'Be careful. They will search all the rooms. Or the owner might come back.'

'Not to this one,' said Sawyer with a smile. 'This pad belonged to Wardle.'

The other man shuddered as he made his way down the stairs towards the lights and the music. This affair had long since passed the boundaries of what he thought of as espionage. He had heard distantly of Tarantyev's prima donna approach; had dismissed much of what he heard as the hyperbole of nostalgia. But now quite clearly any share of control here had passed from him. The kudos, if any, would be Tarantyev's. The most he could hope for was survival.

His politics did not pay much heed to non-earthly affairs, but he said a little prayer almost unconsciously as he re-entered the ballroom.

10

*The instant you discover him write to me
immediately . . . If he attempts to run away
from you, knock him down or lock him up. You
have my full authority.*

MR. SAMUEL PICKWICK

Christmas Day dawned, or rather the backcloth of the driving
snow shaded gradually from black to grey and stuck there,
like a pantomime transformation scene gone wrong. The party
started to break up shortly after 2 a.m., though it was a good
two hours before all the guests had retired to their rooms.
Three times Boswell's seven men had gone through Dingley
Dell, working in pairs for safety, with Boswell himself making
up the fourth pair. By the time the guests started going to bed
he had to admit failure. Continuing the search seemed a waste
of time and energy. In addition there was the risk of alerting
the genuine holidaymakers to the fact that something odd was
going on. Even the professionals seemed to have enjoyed
themselves sufficiently to miss most of the comings and goings,
though Boswell knew that in any case they would be too professional to reveal that they had noticed. Only Leclerc, who
had either not been drinking or had a built-in imperviousness

to alcohol, had sought Boswell out on the pretext of some procedural query on the next day's business.

'That's right,' said Boswell, with as much unconcern as he could muster. 'There's a session from ten-thirty until twelve. Then a break for the roast goose and Christmas pud. Followed by another meeting between three-thirty and six, before the evening festivities start.'

'These interruptions for gluttony!' said Leclerc, pursing his lips in disapproval. Then, casually, 'Mr. Wardle, our very. jolly host. He seems to have left us early tonight. Swinburne too.'

'Saving their strength for tomorrow. I mean today,' laughed Boswell.

'Very wise. Pah! that German pig! See how he sweats!'

The wassail perhaps had loosened Leclerc's tongue sufficiently for his prejudices to slide out, thought Boswell, watching the ungainly assent of the stairs by a very red and merry Herr Bear. His wife, impassive as ever, came behind and caught him whenever he fell.

'Good night,' said Leclerc, and walked away before the German could reach them. Suzie had disappeared from the scene completely some time earlier. Clearly the implication of what Arabella had seen (if he could believe her account) was that the Frenchwoman knew of the injury to Stephen Swinburne. But it would have to wait till morning now.

Mrs. Hislop had listened in disbelieving silence to Boswell's suggestion that Stephen's injury was the result of an accidental fall. But she seemed ready to comply with his request for silence on the matter for the sake of the other guests.

'He should be all right, I think,' she said. 'Call me if you need me. Otherwise I'm just an ordinary guest.'

She had then gone off to look into her uncle's room to check that he was all right. Boswell had walked with her along the corridor and as she entered Bloodworth's room after a perfunctory knock, he glanced over her shoulder into the interior.

What he saw took him by surprise. Sitting on the edge of the bed in deep conversation with the man was Arabella.

Ridiculously, as he walked away, his main feeling was one

of jealousy. There had been something very intimate about the scene. His mind began to piece together fragmentary hypotheses in which Arabella and Bloodworth were fellow-agents, old friends, lovers even—though he kept well away from that one. How old was the fellow? and how sick? It made useful cover, illness. You were upstairs while everyone else was downstairs. Very handy.

The matter was still very much on his mind when he appeared for his interview with Swinburne. It was short and fairly nasty, in a civilised kind of way. Swinburne listened to Boswell's account of matters in silence, then announced it was his rule never to interfere with the work of operatives in the field. On the other hand, it was also his rule that incompetence received short shrift. He would expect, in the short term, solutions; in the longer term, flawless security arrangements.

'I never liked this Dingley Dell idea much,' he said finally. 'I was persuaded against my judgment.'

'We all pay for our moments of weakness,' said Boswell stolidly.

It was a sour note on which to end a sour interview. This and fatigue in part accounted for the acrimony with which he greeted Arabella whom he met a few minutes later walking down the corridor to her new room.

She smiled rather wanly at him, but all he could manage in reply was, 'Is the old man tired out then?'

'So you still spy on me,' she said levelly.

'You flatter yourself. We watch everything suspicious.'

'And I am suspicious?'

'Certainly. At least, your actions are.'

'Is visiting a sick man suspicious?'

'Sick!' said Boswell contemptuously. 'How sick is sick, I wonder. I suppose it was you who put him on to the peephole?'

'I suppose it was. He spends a lot of time in his bedroom. He deserves to have his privacy respected. We all do.'

'Privacy! If we had respected privacy a bit less, Wardle might still be alive,' he said accusingly.

'That's not fair,' she answered, flushed with anger.

'No. Being dead's never fair.'

He walked away. Another sour note to end on. And it had brought him no nearer to solving the problem of Bloodworth. If there were a problem. Perhaps he was going out of his way to look for problems? He didn't know. All he knew was that Wardle was dead. The following winter would have seen him safely retired. Now he was at the bottom of a pond. It was too dangerous to attempt to recover his body in the dark. So there he must lie. And why? God knows what Sawyer (it *must* have been Sawyer) hoped to achieve, no matter who he was working for. Information obtained *via* espionage was only useful as long as the enemy did not know of the leak. Advance knowledge of a new European security set-up would be invaluable, but at this stage in negotiations discreet observation was the only sensible mode of work.

Either the man was very incompetent or, and this was far worse, he preferred to work like this. It could be that he was the same fellow who had blasted Custer, the groom, on the hillside. Another unnecessary death, like Wardle's? The fellow seemed almost to invite discovery.

At this point Boswell had yawned suddenly and hugely. He was very tired. The strain and tensions were beginning to tell. Presumably wherever Sawyer was now he was resting at his ease. It was time he did the same. And so to bed. And so Christmas Day dawned.

People greet Christmas Day in a variety of moods and situations. The religious, and quite a number of the non-religious, see it arrive from the vantage point of large vaulted, domed, galleried, towered, spired buildings which either decorum or economy has preserved from central heating. Major Herbert Halloway was one of these. He knelt by his small, comfortable wife who accepted without complaint all the alarums and excursions which his trade involved, and for whose sake, whenever possible, he accompanied her to their unlovely Victorian parish church. But this was as far as he could accompany her. Internally, his sights were fixed not on the promise of heaven but the comfort of bed. The only Christian thought which entered his mind was the hope that the nineteenth century was being kinder to Wardle and Boswell than the church architects had been to the present congregation. And the only prayer that he uttered, but this most fervently, was that the two aforementioned gentleman should so organise their Christmas Day that no calls would be made upon Major Herbert Halloway.

Others, more or less fortunate than the major, fall into bed full of good cheer and expensive drink and are awoken at a time in the morning commensurate with the degree of diplomacy they have instilled into their children. Everyone gets what he deserves at Christmas.

Though some, of course, feel they are getting less than their share. If, for instance, you are a fifty-year-old ginger-bearded tramp, waking up in a draughty, scarcely furnished and completely unheated, room, you may feel that your portion of life's goodies have somehow been misdirected. But philosophy helps. Who knows what joys the day might bring?

Others, apparently much better placed in the grand scheme of things, may have found sleep has evaded them as they lie in their warm comfortable beds. Some sudden shock—a boy half-dead for instance—might have called into doubt a whole course of action. And the steady breathing of the man at your side brings little comfort.

Or some sudden, astounding discovery might have climaxed a day of startling activity and be warring in a young woman's head with the desire to analyse and assess the beginnings of what she feels could be an important relationship.

Sleep is by no means the reward of the just. It is very possible for a man who has committed murder on Christmas Eve and who, if the occasion arises, intends to commit murder on Christmas Day, to sleep as soundly as a well-nurtured child.

And a great deal more soundly than one who, though age and health and all things in him crave for sleep, feels it necessary for the duty he owes his employers to rise in the grey light of dawn and, Grendel-like, tread a stealthy path to rooms where other sleepers lie.

And finally there is another strange band of people who rise on this most holy of days and, laying no claim even to symbolic justification, make their way to a variety of river banks and sea-shores, where they hurl themselves, shrieking with

93

pain and amazement at their own foolhardiness, into the icy water. Such a band met on the stony foreshore near Southend-on-Sea. Some minutes later one woman emerged from the water clutching something in her hands. For some time, in the general outcry from the bathers, her own shrieks went unnoticed.

Boswell came out of the grey depths swiftly and completely within a single second of the hand's touching his shoulder. But he kept his eyes closed and his breathing steady until the voice whispered urgently once more, 'Mr. Boswell!'

It was Johnson. He sat up.

'What's on?' he asked.

'There's someone moving around downstairs.'

He was out of bed, pulling on clothes, in an instant.

'Where?'

'In the hall. Trying the front door.'

Boswell grunted happily. No one was getting out of the front door tonight—not without a combination of three keys or a charge of gelignite.

'Who's watching?'

'Joe and Dave. Like you said, we haven't made contact.'

'Good.'

He wanted to know what this man Sawyer was trying to do. And he wanted to be sure he was taken with no further injury to anyone else.

At the bottom of the stairs they met the Fat Boy.

'He's in there,' he whispered, nodding towards the parlour door. 'We think he's trying the windows. He seems keen to get out.'

What for, Boswell couldn't imagine. A glance out of his bedroom window before he came down had shown him that the wind and snow were still dancing together with as much abandon as ever. He very much doubted now if Colley could have got through. Or, even if he had, there was little anyone could do in these conditions.

Still, once they got hold of the man in there, the situation would be perfectly in control. He put aside his concern for Colley's well-being and concentrated on the job in hand.

'Where's Dave?'

'He's gone out of the back and round the side of the house just in case our man does get out.'

'Fine. Have you had a good look at the fellow yet? Is it Sawyer?'

Joe shook his head.

'Can't say. He's well muffled up. He'll need to be if he's going out in this weather!'

'Which he isn't. He'll have a hell of a job opening those windows. They're all individually locked. Right, let's go and get him. Johnson, you stay by the door. Joe, you go left. I'll switch on the lights and go right. Keep low and find cover. There's a big settee in the corner, make for that. He might start shooting.'

Carefully, they advanced to the door. It was slightly ajar, which made things easier. The light switches were in the wall to the right, concealed behind an anti-draught curtain in keeping with the Dingley Dell policy of having all mod cons present, but unobtrusive.

It was a policy which had its disadvantages in the present circumstances.

'Go,' said Boswell, and plunged through the door. His right hand, outstretched to flick down the light-switches, became entangled in the curtain and long, precious seconds were lost as he disentangled himself and located the switch panel. If Sawyer started blasting off at the door now, it could be nasty.

But when the light finally spilled down from the pseudo-candelabra, and Boswell hurled himself full length behind a chair, it seemed as if Sawyer had used the time for other purposes.

Halfway down the room, a long velvet curtain fluttered eerily in front of an open window.

'Damn and blast!' swore Boswell, picking himself up and making for it, Joe close behind him.

'Where the hell is he?' said Joe peering out into the swirling snow. 'Wait! There!'

A dark shape appeared out of the whiteness.

'No,' said Boswell. 'That's Dave. In any case . . .'

He was noticing what should have immediately jumped out and hit him in the eye. There was no sign of any disturbance in the snow outside the window. Which meant that . . .

Behind them came a thud and a startled cry. They turned. Johnson, tempted by the lack of violent activity within to step through the door, lay on his side on the floor. His hand was grasping the back of his neck. A raincoated figure was glimpsed briefly through the doorway, moving fast and heading for the stairs. A still fluttering curtain by the window nearest the side-wall revealed his hiding place.

'Come on,' said Boswell. He jumped over the still, prostrate figure of Johnson and sprinted from the room. Halfway up the stairs, the fugitive presented an easy target, but he was reluctant to shoot. The man seemed to be moving very slowly and should be easily overtaken. On the landing he put on a bit of a spurt, but Boswell was now close behind.

It wasn't even worth calling on him to stop. He was moving at what was scarcely a quick walk now, more of a stagger. He just made it round the angle of the corridor and when Boswell turned the corner the man was on his knees by the wall, sliding slowly sideways. Boswell halted and watched. Further down the corridor a door opened. He looked up. It was Arabella, glorious in a skimpy nightdress, who was running towards him. This concern for his well-being was very touching. But there might still be danger.

'Keep back!' he commanded, looking down at the man who was now lying flat on his face.

Arabella ignored him, stopping only when she reached the man on the floor. She knelt beside him and gently turned him over so that his head rested on her lap.

It came as no surprise to Boswell to see who it was. Face grey as ash, breathing intermittent and harsh, it was Bloodworth. If he had had any doubts about the genuineness of the man's illness, they were dispersed now.

Arabella looked up at him, her eyes full of contemptuous accusation.

'You bastard,' she said. 'You've killed him.'

11

*You are a humbug, sir . . . I will speak plainer
if you wish it. An impostor, sir.*

MR. SAMUEL PICKWICK

Breakfast was a remarkably lively meal, indecently, so it
seemed, to those who had had less than their fair share of
sleep the previous night.

There was a feeling of excitement among the guests as they
realised they were to all intents and purposes cut off from the
outside world. Many were disappointed that they were unable
to make or receive Christmas greeting telephone calls, but the
sense of being involved in an adventure (safely and comfortably endured) more than compensated.

After breakfast people drifted into the parlour, where they
were delighted to discover heaps of gifts piled beneath the
Christmas tree, and even more delighted to find how well
chosen they had been.

'It might have been hand-picked, specially for me!' averred
Mrs. Burton, looking at the small bottle of perfume she had
just received. 'You're very efficient, Mr. Boswell. You must
have a file on me somewhere!'

Boswell nodded his appreciation of the compliment and of
the unconscious irony. The investigation carried out on all

97

the guests had proved very useful in selecting their gifts. It seemed, however, it had been less useful in its premier task of weeding out security risks. It might well turn out that there was some innocent explanation of Bloodworth's activities early in the morning, but it would be foolish to assume anything but the worst. The old man had been treated by his niece, Mrs. Hislop, and put to bed. His condition was not as grave as it had appeared to Boswell at first, but the doctor had made it clear he was a very sick man and it was out of the question for him to talk. Of course, her own close connection with Bloodworth made her opinion less weighty than it might otherwise have been, but it was impossible to contradict it without alternative medical advice. And certainly Boswell's own amateur observations confirmed her diagnosis.

There had been no opportunity to talk with Arabella since her outburst. Her own interest in Bloodworth was still as mysterious as the man's activities themselves. But there were other matters of greater concern. Sawyer, first and foremost. Incredibly, there was still no sign of the man. He must have got away out of the house, Boswell decided. Perhaps Bloodworth had had some kind of rendezvous with him? But even this theory was hard to maintain. He had detached four of the seven men under his control and sent them through the snow to give the barn and stables a thorough going-over.

The result was nothing.

Perhaps Sawyer had tried to make his escape in the night. In which case there was little doubt that nature would have done Boswell's work for him and be holding the fugitive to be picked up later when the thaw came. Dead.

It would simplify matters. And, recalling Wardle, Boswell had no qualms about hoping that this in fact was what had happened.

Wardle's absence he explained (and continually, painfully, had to re-explain to a succession of guests) as the result of illness, a temporary indisposition brought on by the previous evening's festivities. The laughs and witticisms the explanation produced were hard to bear. But bear them he had to, especially now Wardle's mantle of the jovial mine host had fallen onto his shoulders. Fortunately the hotel staff were easy to cope with. They were not trained field operatives in the way that Joe and Johnson and the others were. But they were all hand-picked after strict vetting for qualities of discretion and trustworthiness. Their salaries were rather more than the going rate for their respective jobs and they did not need to be told that over-curiosity or garrulousness would more rapidly result in loss of place than the mere spilling of hot soup down a guest's cleavage. They accepted Boswell's story of Wardle's indisposition as unquestioningly as the guests. But unlike the guests they would know, or very soon discover, that Wardle was not resting peacefully in his bed.

Boswell could only hope that none of their kitchen speculations came anywhere near the truth. A couple of extra pound notes in your pay packet didn't buy loyalty in the face of sudden death.

As he came from the kitchen, one of the maids followed him with a breakfast tray.

'Who's that for?' he asked casually.

'Madame Leclerc, the French lady,' said the woman. 'Not feeling well, I hear. Seems to be catching, sir.'

He didn't respond to her hint of irony but took the tray from her.

'I'm going upstairs,' he said. 'I'll see she gets it.'

He had noticed Leclerc a few minutes earlier going into the dining room. The next conference session was due to start in about twenty minutes. It was time he could usefully spend having a quiet word with Suzie.

She showed no surprise when he walked into her room with the tray. She did not look as if she had slept much. There were large dark shadows under her eyes. Her hair hung uncombed round her unpowdered face. She was sitting up in bed smoking a foul-smelling cigarette and her nightdress had slipped low on her shoulders. She made no effort to adjust it, but stared at him gloomily, unblinkingly, through a cloud of blue smoke. It was like a scene from one of those magnificent French gangster films they didn't seem to make any more.

He put the tray down on the bedside table.

'I'm sorry you are unwell,' he said.

She shrugged, dislodging the nightdress a little more. The

action, he diagnosed with a tinge of regret, was accidental; the display of such a breathtaking canyon of cleavage arose from complete indifference rather than any desire to distract him from his purpose.

'I'd like to ask you a few questions if I may,' he began.

'Does my husband know you are here?' she interrupted.

'No,' he answered. 'Shall I send for him?'

'No,' she said, shaking her head.

'You know, of course, what your husband is doing here?'

It was a rhetorical question. Some security men kept their wives in complete and lifelong ignorance of the nature of their work. A wise move, if at all possible. But Suzie Leclerc had been actively concerned in the business herself when she and her husband-to-be met. After their marriage she had retired from active work while Jules had progressed from strength to strength in the department. But it was inconceivable that she was here without full knowledge of what was going on.

She nodded.

'Then you'll realise how important it is that I investigato anything unusual.'

'Yes.'

'Good. In that case, I'd like you to tell me exactly what happened after you left the ball last night with Stephen Swinburne.'

She reached out of bed to the tray and poured herself a cup of coffee. The movement did nothing to help Boswell's peace of mind. She was a beautifully made woman.

She drank her coffee. He had the feeling that she was on the brink of telling him the truth. She leaned forward and almost unconsciously he took a small step backwards.

The realisation seemed to dawn on her then of his interest in her attractions. A look of distaste, whether for him or for herself he could not say, passed over her face and she pulled up the coverlet round her neck.

'You are mistaken,' she said. 'Young Mr. Swinburne and I may have left the room at the same time but we did not leave together.'

'Why did you leave?' he asked.

'Why? I wished to go to the bathroom. You want details?'

'The bathroom. I see. Not the linen room? You didn't go into the linen room?'

She was taken aback for a moment, then she laughed, not very successfully.

'Why should I go to the, what did you call it, this linen room?'

'You want details?' echoed Boswell, mockingly.

She looked at him angrily.

'Details? All right. You give me these details!' she snapped.

'I too should like to hear these details,' said a new voice.

Boswell turned. Standing just inside the door was Leclerc.

Boswell knew he had missed whatever opportunity he had had to learn anything from Suzie.

'Good morning, monsieur,' he said. 'I just brought your wife's breakfast tray and we were discussing some details of last night's party. But it was really you I came to fetch. I am sure you do not want to be late for this morning's conference session?'

Leclerc returned his smile.

'Of course not, Monsieur Boswell,' he said. 'You are most solicitous. Let us go together, shall we? We will meet at lunch, my dear.'

They left the room together and made their way in silence towards the conference area where all was in readiness and most of the other delegates were already present.

'Good morning, Leclerc,' said Swinburne suavely. 'We should be able to make good progress today, I hope.'

'I hope so too,' answered Leclerc. 'Are we ready to start?'

'Everyone's here except Herr Himmelstor, I think,' said Swinburne. 'As soon as he comes, we'll begin. But it would be discourteous to start without him.'

They had to wait nearly another fifteen minutes before Herr Bear appeared, rather pale and still wearing his military uniform. He clicked his heels and gave a short stiff bow to the already seated delegates, then disappeared into the bar next door and returned clutching what Boswell later discovered to be half a pint of hock and soda-water. Whether it did him any good, Boswell did not immediately discover, as his attention was caught by urgent signals from Joe standing in the doorway.

'What's up?' he asked in a low voice.

'It's Sawyer. We've found him.'

'Great! Where've you put him?'

'Well, nowhere,' said Joe, rather unhappily.

'What the hell do you mean? Where is he?'

Joe smiled conciliatingly.

'He's in the parlour. Drinking coffee.'

'He's what!'

He realised he had unconsciously raised his voice. Glancing back into the conference room, he saw Swinburne looking at him speculatively. Giving him a reassuring smile, he closed the door and turned on the Fat Boy.

'Show me!' he snarled.

He was somewhat reassured to see James and Grose, the two 'gamekeepers', standing casually outside the parlour.

'Johnson's covering the window outside,' said James.

'Fine,' said Boswell. 'Play it cool now. We don't want anyone in there getting hurt. Let's go.'

He stepped into the parlour.

And stopped.

Prepared though he was for it, the sight took his breath away. Robert E. Lee Sawyer, who the day before had probably blown a man's stomach open with a shotgun, held another's head beneath icy water till the life bubbled away from him, and possibly clubbed a nineteen-year-old boy to unconsciousness, perhaps idiocy, was stretched at his ease on a *chaise longue*, the centre of a group of highly amused and entertained dames. Where he had spent the night was still unknown, but clearly he had spent it in some comfort. He was very spruce, freshly shaved and had somehow got access to the hotel's Dickensian wardrobe. The evening wear he had been given for the ball had been discarded and its place taken by a very elegant sporting outfit consisting of a green shooting coat, plaid neckerchief and closely fitted drabs.

He seemed to be in the middle of an autobiographical shaggy-dog story describing how he had found himself driven by a blizzard in the Rockies to take shelter in a single-roomed log-cabin with four women, an Indian guide and an episcopalian minister. His audience, prevented by the snow from venturing outside, were clearly delighted by this diversion.

'So this minister, he says, "Brethren, and sistren, let us kneel down and pray," which we did very willingly, there being nothing more attractive immediately suggesting itself; but after a couple of minutes, when the splinters in the floor started working themselves through my knee-caps, I took a peek between my fingers—like this . . .'

He put his hands up over his face, opened a couple of fingers and squinted through towards Boswell. The ladies giggled appreciatively.

'Well, you'll never believe this, ladies,' he went on. 'But there in the furthermost and darkest corner was that there minister and he was . . . well, I won't say what he was a-doing, but when we finished our prayer, he looked a mighty relieved man!'

There was a great deal of laughter, Sawyer's uninhibited guffaws outsounding everyone else. Under cover of the noise, Boswell moved swiftly down the room and took up a position immediately behind the American. The Fat Boy meanwhile had moved over to the window where he announced loudly and totally inaccurately, 'I think the snow's slackening off.'

There was a general movement towards the window to check on this hypothesis. Boswell leaned over Sawyer, prodded his neck none too gently with the Walther PPK he held in his jacket pocket, and said conversationally, 'I wonder if I might have a moment, Mr. Sawyer? I don't think we got your passport when you arrived. If it would be convenient for you to fetch it now . . .'

He gave another prod, but it was unnecessary. Sawyer stood up, his face a-beam with co-operation, his hands hanging loosely at his sides, well clear of his pockets.

'Sure thing, Boz, old son,' he drawled. 'Hey, girls. I'll finish the story later. It gets worse.'

The women, having seen for themselves how fallacious was Joe's optimism, cooed in disappointment. Boswell too felt irrationally disappointed. Clearly a struggle here with the risk of physical harm to these innocent bystanders would be regarded by Swinburne as a disaster. But for all that something inside him longed for an excuse to see sudden, violent pain remove that open attractive smile from Sawyer's lips and glaze those sparkling eyes.

'After you,' he said, and Sawyer unhesitatingly led the way towards the door.

Now something else deep down began to struggle with his desire to hurt Sawyer. A puzzlement. A worry. This was going very easily. Too easily. What the hell could have possessed the man to offer himself for capture like this? Bravado? An acceptance of the inevitable?

At the parlour door they met Arabella. Her expression changed rapidly from shock at the sight of Sawyer, through puzzlement at seeing him in an apparently friendly relationship with Boswell, to understanding as Boswell jerked his head at her to move aside and dug his concealed automatic so hard into the American's spine that he almost stumbled.

In the hallway James and Grose quickly closed on Sawyer while Boswell watched the stairs and Joe held the parlour door shut. It only took a moment.

'He's clean,' said James, stepping back. Odder and odder. No gun. Still that smile, that confident manner, as if he, Sawyer, were completely in control.

The sooner he got him upstairs behind the steel door which closed the conference area off from the rest of Dingley Dell, the better Boswell would be pleased. His mind was already experimenting with notions that Sawyer might have an accomplice. But who? If someone else had slipped through the net . . . It was small comfort that it had been Wardle's net. It was his now. People like Swinburne didn't have nets. They just sat in great comfort and picked at the bones of perfectly grilled fish.

What was comforting was his personal knowledge of the meticulous nature of the searches all the guests had undergone on arrival. Even the delegates, the only difference between them and the genuine holidaymakers being that the former knew they were being searched. The only people with guns in Dingley Dell were Boswell's men and of them he was one hundred per cent certain. Or ninety-nine. Distrust was the better part of complacency.

For all that he sighed with relief as the metal door closed behind him and Sawyer was pushed into a small lounge in the company of three men, each quite keen to kill him.

'Just don't let him move,' he said. 'If he does, shoot a hole in his knee.'

He put the teasing problem of Sawyer's motives out of his mind as he made for the conference room. It was silly to play chess when you could be playing tiggy with hammers. As long as you held the hammer. All he had to do now was tell Swinburne. Let him play chess if he wanted to. He, Boswell, would merely keep Sawyer safe. Dead if need be, but safe. He and his little force of seven men. We are seven. He chuckled to himself. And three of us with Sawyer dwell; James, Grose and Joe. One is servicing the conference room; Dave, the coach-guard. One is up aloft in the attic; Alf, the driver. One is on duty at the metal door; Anderson. Which leaves one outside still; Johnson.

A fairly formidable band. And as soon as this damned snow gave up, reinforcements would arrive whether he wanted them or not. Colley may have got through, or at least be well placed to get through quickly once the weather changed. But even without Colley's report it was certain some kind of investigatory action would be taken. They must be getting worried out there at the silence surrounding Dingley Dell. Possibly some poor bastards had already been dragged from the bosom of their families this Christmas morning and were at present ploughing their reluctant way towards the hotel.

Swinburne came out of the conference room quickly in response to a note from Boswell. He greeted the news of Sawyer's capture with a small nod, as though confirming to himself the accuracy of his own strategy. Boswell's difficulty in interpreting the situation was also treated as something to be expected.

'You've got seven men, and yourself,' he said coldly. 'Five up here, you and one other below with the guests. And one outside. In the stables perhaps. Always cover your outside, Boswell. Think you can manage it?'

Only the memory of the man's son, lying pale and unconscious in Arabella's bed, prevented Boswell from replying concisely and forcibly. He stuck at conciseness.

'Yes, sir,' he said.

'This man Sawyer. Watch him, of course. But no questioning. No conversation even. I want him unspoilt for the experts.'

'Yes, sir.'

'Good. I'd better get back in there.'

'Everything going all right?' ventured Boswell. A frosty smile touched the thin lips and momentarily the man became almost human.

'Fine. If only it weren't for these damn' foreigners.'

Boswell smiled in return and held his smile till the conference-room door closed behind Swinburne. He wished he could believe that the joke was nothing more than a joke. But everything in his own experience told him that there were few things more chauvinistic than national security agencies. Information which Foreign Secretaries might exchange over cocktails at a reception was hoarded as protectively as the most sacrosanct defence secrets. It worked both ways. On several occasions information had been obtained at a high price—sometimes financial, sometimes human—only for the proud agent to discover his masters in Whitehall already knew the greater part of it.

The kind of security union which Boswell hoped might evolve out of Europe's economic unity had a long hard road ahead of it. He pushed aside the thought which had started forming in his mind with increasing frequency in the last twenty-four hours that perhaps the delegates next door were by no means the best equipped for the job in hand. If the present operation was ballsed up, God knows when those ruthless, hard-thinking men could be brought together in one place again.

Perhaps that had been Sawyer's aim, or the aim of his masters whom Boswell now automatically assumed to be the KGB. Perhaps one of the other Eastern European countries. The CIA would be just as interested in the Dingley Dell operation, but the agency would never play it so rough with their

NATO allies. Not if there was any chance of being caught at it, that was.

But even the disruption-by-Russia theory did not really ring true. Observation and infiltration would have been much more useful—and typical for that matter. Perhaps the old rivalry between the KGB and the GRU had taken a new form. There had been several reports from America in the past few years of espionage activities becoming suddenly and alarmingly *active*. Sabotage. Assassinations. Stuff for the cinema! A name had been mentioned, but it escaped him. Worth checking later.

If this snow ever let up sufficiently for anyone to get out or in! he thought gloomily.

He checked back to see all was well with the three men looking after Sawyer.

'I want two of you in here at all times,' he said. He produced a piece of chalk and drew a line on the floor.

'If he crosses that line, shoot him. And you don't cross it either. Understood?'

They nodded and he left. As an afterthought he brought Alf down from the attic and sat him on a chair outside the room in which Sawyer was being held.

'Any disturbance in there,' he said, 'You don't go in. You wait here and see who comes out. OK?'

Alf nodded. A cheerful red-cheeked countryman, he was type-cast in his role as the weather-braving, horse-controlling Dickensian coach-driver. But he was a wicked man with a gun and his cheeriness stopped at his eyes.

Slightly happier at the thought that Sawyer at least was safely out of the way, Boswell left the conference suite and went to Arabella's former room to check if Stephen had recovered consciousness yet. Besides his genuine concern with the boy's health, he was eager to hear what he could tell of the attack on him. It seemed as motiveless as the rest of Sawyer's activities. Unless, and his mind kept on returning uneasily to this qualification, unless they weren't all Sawyer's activities; an ambiguous form of words without much comfort in either part of the ambiguity.

To his surprise, Arabella was there, despite the presence

by the bedside of one of the hotel staff, a large, comfortable woman who had had some experience of nursing as a girl during the war.

'I'm just collecting the rest of my gear,' said Arabella in explanation. After her outburst the previous night she seemed to have withdrawn to a position of armed neutrality.

'Fine. How's young Swinburne?'

'He seems to be much better. Mrs. Hislop was here a few moments ago. What she said in simple terms was that he has passed out of a state of unconsciousness into one of deep sleep. At least I think that's what she said. Anyway, the longer this goes on, the better at the moment, until he can be got into a hospital.'

'That's good,' said Boswell. 'The minute this snow gives up, we'll get things arranged. Can I help you with anything?'

'Thanks,' said Arabella, festooning him generously with a selection of garments, some of which he was certain one or two of the more ancient dons at his college would scarcely believe to exist.

As he laid them on the bed in her new room, Arabella said casually, 'So you found Sawyer?'

'Not exactly,' smiled Boswell ruefully. 'More precisely, he let himself be found.'

Briefly he described what had happened. He was still far from the stage where he could possibly discountenance Arabella as Sawyer's hypothetical ally, but this only made the appearance of complete confidence all the more essential. Or perhaps he just wanted to thaw her coldness.

'What happens now?' she asked next.

'We'll keep him under very close guard until the weather breaks. Then we'll ship him out of here as fast as we can.'

'Where to? The village bobby's back kitchen?'

'Somewhere a little more discreet than that, I should imagine. It will all be done very quietly.'

'And me?' she asked challengingly. 'Will I be swept under some special mat too?'

'I see no reason for that,' replied Boswell. 'Not if you co-operate.'

'And how should I co-operate?'

'To start with, perhaps you could tell me all you know about Bloodworth. That might help.'

'Why, certainly, Mr. Boswell,' she answered sweetly. 'He's an old man suffering from a heart condition exacerbated by being chased round the hotel by a gang of hoodlums waving guns. Shouldn't you be taking notes?'

'You know him, don't you?'

'*You* know everything. You tell me.'

'All right. I will if you like. I've had a long talk with Mrs. Hislop and she's proved much more co-operative.'

It was a feeble bluff. His attempts to cross-question the woman doctor had proved even more unsuccessful than his present conversation with Arabella, who was laughing whole-heartedly. At least it was an aesthetically pleasing reaction. He found himself joining in.

'I'd better go and get the thumbscrews,' he said finally. At least the atmosphere in the room was no longer as metaphorically chilly as when he entered.

'Just one thing,' he said. 'If you *are* on our side, make sure you're not doing anything—or leaving anything undone—which could cause harm. Bullets don't ask questions.'

He turned to go now.

'Hang on,' she said. 'You'd better have these.'

From beneath her pillow she produced a small pile of loose papers and handed them over.

He riffled through them quickly, then at a slower pace.

'Where did you get these?' he asked calmly.

'They were lying around when I found Stephen last night.'

'You know what they are?'

'Yes,' she said. 'Records of the conference sessions. Details of proposals. Facts, figures. Not very interesting really.'

'Why didn't you give them to me last night?'

'I hadn't had a chance to read them, had I?' she answered pertly. 'And later I didn't feel in a very giving mood as far as you were concerned.'

'You acted wrongly,' he said. 'Both times. Especially the second time. Personal feelings have got to be kept out of this.'

'I'll remember that,' said Arabella, looking at him ironically. 'Before you stalk off in your cloak and dagger, though, here's something else for your collection. Stephen's, I presume. I found it in the wardrobe.'

She tossed a small metal badge on to the garment-strewn bed. It fell on a pair of tiger-striped knickers and Boswell let it lie there while he examined it in silence. It was in the form of a bronze olive leaf with the initials I.P. on it in green enamel.

'I.P.' said Boswell meditatively.

'InterPax,' said Arabella. 'The student pressure group for international peace.'

'A worthy cause,' said Boswell.

'Crap!' snorted Arabella. 'We both know where their finance comes from.'

Well, I certainly do, thought Boswell. But how do you? He picked up the badge and put it in his pocket.

'Find anything else?' he asked noncommittally.

'Just a sex-guidance manual evidently written for contortionists. Have you spoken to Madame Leclerc yet?'

It was a nice juxtapositioning of ideas, offered completely deadpan. But two could play at that.

'Yes,' he said. 'Don't forget dinner's at twelve. You'd better go along to the gown room.'

He looked critically at her slacks and ski-sweater.

'Christ!' she said. 'You mean it all goes on, the charade? Yes, I suppose it would. I suppose if the charade ever stopped, people like you would be out of a job.'

'Excuse me now,' he said politely. 'People like me have work to do.'

He wasn't merely being ironic. There was indeed a great deal to do. Well trained though the staff were, someone had to check that arrangements for the noontide Christmas dinner were in train. This, coupled with frequent appeals to his Dickensian expertise, kept him busy for a solid hour and it was twenty to twelve before he found a breathing space. Beckoning Johnson to follow him, he stepped out into the front porch of Dingley Dell.

The snow had drifted high here, six feet or more on some parts of the front of the house, though the blizzard had gusted

110

too erratically to produce any consistency of drift. Now the wind had almost died away, though the snow still fell; large, soft Christmas-card flakes floating gently down, completely lacking in menace. One or two of the guests had boldly ventured out, only to admit defeat after a few yards. It had taken very energetic shovel work to clear a path through to the stables so that the horses could be fed. A surrealistic white shape beside the stables puzzled Boswell for a while until he realised it was the tractor used to haul tree-trunks down from the hillside.

The sight annoyed him. It should have been put away the night before. It was no longer just a question of authenticity; the vehicle might have been able to get through the snow to the village, but now it would probably be impossible to start it! Still, even tractors could hardly negotiate six-foot snowdrifts.

'Shall I try to get through?' asked Johnson, peering up at the sky.

'Not now!' said Boswell. 'Colley's out there somewhere already. Wait till it stops, then at least your tracks won't be filling in behind you. We'll have our Christmas dinner first.'

He glanced at his watch.

'It's time they were coming down,' he said. 'Let's go and hurry them up. And I want you to stay up there. Right?'

His strategy was simple. During dinner everyone would be together where he could keep an eye on them. If anyone did slip through the net and make an attempt to get Sawyer out, there would be seven well armed and efficiently trained men waiting for him.

When he returned to the conference area he discovered the morning session had already broken up. Some of the delegates hurried off to change for dinner with token protests about the inconvenience of having to resume their Dickensian dress. A few, like Herr Bear, had kept their costumes on and now made their way straight downstairs to join the other guests in the parlour for a pre-dinner drink. Boswell felt a little concerned lest any of the genuine guests, forced by the inclement weather to stay together indoors, might have wondered at the

111

absence and mass reappearance of the delegates. But this was the least of his worries at the moment.

He issued a final instruction to his men.

'No one gets in here but me. Understand? No one!'

Then he put on his *maître-d'hôtel* smile and descended to the parlour.

The wassail bowl had appeared once more. Glasses were being filled and emptied at a rate surpassing that even of the previous night. The Yule log on the fire at the kitchen end crackled and sparkled, reflecting heat and light from the red floor-tiles. From the kitchen beyond drifted all the smells of Christmas, some spicy, some pungent, with the unmistakable odour of roasting goose predominant.

The hotel guests, now very much at ease in their borrowed robes, laughed and chattered like old friends. The whole atmosphere was so filled with good cheer and cordiality that Boswell felt himself strangely touched. The lines from *Pickwick Papers* came into his mind. *It was the season of hospitality, merriment, and open-heartedness; the old year was preparing, like an ancient philosopher, to call his friends around him, and amidst the sound of feasting and revelry to pass gently and calmly away. Gay and merry was the time . . .*

Suddenly, hollowly, the dinner gong sounded in the hall. Feeling he was no longer playing a part, he stepped forward, clapped his hands and shouted, 'Ladies, gentleman. My friends! Our poor board awaits your attention. Take your ladies on your arm, gentlemen, and with good cheer and love in your hearts lead them through into the dining room.'

With a great deal of laughter and movement, the guests began to sort themselves out. There was a pause, with no one wishing to be the first to make a move. Then suddenly Mrs. Burton, jolly as ever, darted forward and, much to Boswell's surprise, kissed him on the cheek. There was a general laugh. Looking up he realised that a large bunch of mistletoe hung right above his head.

'Come on, father,' said Mrs. Burton to her smiling husband. 'Don't let dinner get cold!'

Arm in arm they passed through the door. Given this lead, the rest readily followed, almost all the women, much to Boswell's embarrassment, pausing to kiss him. Suzie Leclerc, however, merely glanced scornfully at him, and Frau Cow, her eyes fixed firmly ahead, marched stoutly by. Mrs. Swinburne, looking a little happier at the news of her son's improvement, kissed him warmly. She at least was not blaming him for the attack on the boy. Arabella would have been content to brush his cheek, but when he turned his head so that their lips met, she did not draw back.

Mrs. Hislop was the last through the door. She was unescorted and he offered her his arm.

'How's your uncle doing?' he asked politely.

'He certainly doesn't feel up to Christmas dinner,' said Mrs. Hislop. 'In any case, he wouldn't have eaten till one-fifteen. That's his regular lunch hour.'

She raised her eyebrows slightly as she spoke—enough, with Boswell's knowledge of her as the efficient professional woman, to indicate an ironic resignation to the absurdities of age.

All present and correct then, except for Bloodworth. He couldn't really see the old man as any kind of danger, though there was still the oddity of Arabella's interest in him to be explained. But there could be no real danger there. Especially not with his seven aides up above waiting for it.

Up above. The thought did cross his mind as he entered the dining room that it was rather an uneven division of the armed security force of Dingley Dell; seven upstairs with one man, one downstairs with everybody else.

But the thought slid from his mind as he looked along the huge polished oaken table, bright with silver and pewter which threw back the whiteness of the world outside in a clear pure light. Music was enriching the air, the heart-stirring strains of *God Rest Ye Merry Gentlemen* coming from the unlikely instruments of Thomas Traherne and his four Temple-Haunting Martlets. They were playing it straight this time and had dressed for the occasion, a singular improvement, Boswell felt, on their garb of the night before.

Three great tureens of soup stood ready along the sideboard. In the kitchen the final touches were being given to the five huge roast geese soon to be carved up between the thirty guests. The guests sat down noisily in joyful anticipation.

As the last notes of the carol died away, Boswell struck his glass forcefully with a spoon so that the clear bell-like noise rang round the room.

'My friends!' he cried. 'Soon we will eat and be of good cheer. But let us first bow our heads and give thanks for our presence, and that of our friends and loved ones, at this board, remembering especially those we should like to have here but who are distant, or perhaps lost altogether.'

The words weren't in his script, nor would have been in Wardle's. But they came naturally, and he saw no need to keep them in.

All heads were bowed in silence. Outside a few final flakes fell, then the snow also was still. For a moment it was as if the earth itself had paused on its axis.

'Let the festivities commence!' cried Boswell. His eyes met Arabella's as he looked up. She held his gaze with that disconcerting power she had, but he thought he read sympathy and approval there.

Then there was a noise like a small bomb exploding, followed by a shriek. One of the serving maids had dropped a tureen of soup which had burst on the hard floor.

Startled, everyone turned and looked, ready to forgive and forget her clumsiness at this season of the year. But the maid was not concerned with the consequences of her accident. Nor was the accident itself the cause of her scream.

Boswell turned to follow the direction of all eyes. Behind him, holding a Sterling sub-machine gun in his hand about a foot from Boswell's head, was Thomas Traherne. And in each corner of the room, similarly equipped and looking as much at home with the weapons as with a guitar or saxophone, were his four fellow-musicians.

With sickening force there came back to Boswell's mind the realisation that all the help he could hope to muster was one floor above, fixed there by his own firm order not to move without his instruction.

12

There's rummer things than women in this world though, mind you.

THE BAGMAN

'Please, everybody. Be quiet. We want no trouble,' said Traherne with quiet sincerity. His voice had changed. The casual 'flip' tone and expressions of the pop world had disappeared. Even the face which looked out at them from under the proscenium arch of long brown hair seemed older. A man in his thirties, not a youth in his early twenties.

'Sit down please. *Please*.' The voice pleaded, but not from weakness. Just from a genuine reluctance to use the hideous strength at its disposal.

There was a rustling and scraping of chairs as the diners subsided in their places. Boswell looked down the table. Reactions were as might have been expected. No one looked happy, but to the trained eye there was a clearly marked difference between the expressions of the delegates and those of the genuine holidaymakers. The latter looked as much puzzled as anything, still ready to believe that some as yet uninterpretable Dickensian prank was being played. But the delegates looked resigned, blank, or, in the case of Swinburne, whose gaze Boswell avoided, volcanically furious.

'Carry on your dinner. Will you bring the others, Split?'

The youth called Split moved out of the dining room.

'Mr. Boswell. Please come.'

Boswell stood up and followed Traherne from the table into a recess formed by one of the bay windows. A hubbub of noise broke out at the table. Traherne swung round.

'No talking! There must be no talking, or my men will shoot.'

The threat seemed to work, but suddenly Burton, the little Yorkshireman, was on his feet.

'What the hell's going on?' he demanded. 'Is this some kind of joke? I'll want a bloody good explanation if it is. Come on, Mabel. Let's get upstairs and pack. The sooner I get out of this bloody place, the better I'll be pleased.'

His face red with anger, he pushed back his chair. His wife half rose, her expression uncertain. One of the T.H.M. moved his gun to cover them and raised an interrogative eyebrow at Traherne. Boswell stepped forward.

'Please sit down, Mr. Burton,' he said urgently. 'Mrs. Burton, make your husband sit down. It isn't a joke. There's no time to explain now, but, believe me, these men aren't joking!'

Burton stood uncertain, but finally yielded to the physical efforts of his wife, who dragged him back to his seat by main force. A diversion followed. The door opened and the youth, Split, ushered in a procession of kitchen staff, bearing with them the roast geese, and accompanying dishes of the main course. It was a fine sight, a touch of Old England.

'Now everybody eat! Enjoy yourselves. Only no talking! No moving!'

Places were found for the kitchen and serving staff. The irrepressible Burton suddenly broke out again.

'Well, bugger it! I'm going to enjoy my dinner!'

Pushing aside his soup-plate, he pulled a goose towards him and began carving at the leg. Many of the others began to follow suit and soon the scene achieved something like normality.

'Nice bit of egalitarianism, said Boswell nodding towards the kitchen staff who were tucking in with a special will.

'It takes a gun in this country,' said Traherne. 'Talking of guns, let me have yours.'

Without protest, Boswell produced his Walther and handed it over.

'Now listen carefully to what I have to say. There are thirty people here. Some we know are professionals and as such they are by definition prepared to take their chances. But these others are innocents on holiday. Their lives are your responsibility. Unless Mr. Sawyer and the seven men with him are down here, unarmed, in ten minutes, my men will start shooting.'

Boswell wondered if he meant it. He did not seem the kind of man who would very willingly kill. But then until five minutes ago he had seemed nothing more than the leader of a pop group.

'I suppose you brought the guns in with your instruments?' he said irrelevantly.

'Of course. You have been very poorly organised here, Mr. Boswell.'

It was a professional judgement, an impersonal reproof. But just, very just. Boswell nodded.

'And you too, Mr. Traherne. I am surprised there is need for this.'

He glanced round the room. He was genuinely surprised. T.T. and T.T.H.M. must have been a tremendous cover. A spy-cell on the move! Perfect for picking up or dropping information. He shuddered at the thought of how many important parties and receptions their immaculate credentials had got them into. He himself had studied their file. There had been several brief continental tours. Christ! They must have been better than the GPO.

And now it was all blown. And for what? He thought he saw a shadow pass over Traherne's face.

'We do what we must. Now if you please I'll take you to a phone. Just tell your men to come down. Spell it out to them, Mr. Boswell. Leave no room for subtleties or heroics.'

Boswell shrugged resignedly and glanced across to where Swinburne, his face composed now in a mask of studied indifference, sat picking at the food on his plate. There was no

117

help there. There was no help anywhere unless . . . He glanced out of the window. The snow had definitely stopped. Someone would surely be en route to check that all was well.

Traherne seemed to read his thoughts.

'Now, Mr. Boswell. Or shall we shoot someone as an earnest of our faith?'

'What a nicely spoken spy you are,' mocked Boswell. But he walked across the room, Traherne close behind, and went to the telephone concealed behind a large vase in the hallway. Everyone except Burton stopped eating to watch him go.

'Hello, Johnson?' he said. 'Boswell here. Listen carefully. We've got trouble. Yes, down here. More than we can handle without a lot of people getting hurt. Here's what you do. Leave your guns up there, come out together with Sawyer and bring him down here.'

He now listened for a while. Traherne's gun barrel rose till it fitted snugly under his chin.

'No,' he said with difficulty. 'Nothing, try nothing. You understand? Just bring Sawyer down here.'

Gently he replaced the receiver.

'Thank you,' said Traherne. 'Now, back inside. Split!'

The youth called Split came to meet them and after a few whispered instructions from Traherne, went out. They heard him climbing the stairs. Boswell found himself guided back to his place. He sat down studiously avoiding catching anyone's eyes though he felt every gaze boring into him, some accusingly, some (he hoped) sympathetically. But not many. Even the genuine guests seemed to have made up their minds that their search for someone to blame for current events ended with him.

There was a noise outside, approaching footsteps. Then with a flamboyantly theatrical gesture, Sawyer stepped into the room.

But his entry was spoilt almost immediately. Behind him there was a sudden flurry of movement accompanied almost instantly by a shot. A cry of pain and anger. Running feet. Two of the other Martlets leapt to the doorway. Split's voice. 'He's making for the front!'

Unthinkingly Boswell stood up from his seat and moved

118

into the window recess. From the bay he had a clear view of the front door.

Even as he looked, it burst open and Dave, the coach-guard, hurled himself out. In his hand was a small automatic. Whether it was his own idea or a plan conceived by all of them, Boswell did not know. Probably the former, it was so insane, so risky to everyone. A concealed gun, a break near the door. Then a ten-mile journey through deep snow to the village.

For what? It was mad, mad! But it was action and Boswell found himself willing the ruddy-faced man on as he headed for the shelter of the barn and the trees beyond.

He might have made it if it hadn't been for the snow. It deepened where it banked up against the white-swathed tractor. It was like watching a bather running into the sea. Suddenly the feet could not be raised above the surface of the snow; resistance doubled, trebled, as impetus was lost. Even then he might have made it before pursuit reached the door. But Boswell felt himself shouldered roughly aside. Sawyer peered through the window, wrested Traherne's machine gun from his hand, crashed the barrel through the glass panes and fired instantly. One long burst.

Professionally Boswell noted the perfection of his aim. There was no wasteful, telltale powdering of snow as he found his range. Only an almost imperceptible jerking of cloth in an area of about nine inches between Dave's shoulder blades. Down he went without even a spasm of agony. The snow was so deep and soft that it almost swallowed him up.

Seconds later one of Traherne's men came out of the house. He paused while he took in what had happened, then approached the body with unnecessary caution. Sawyer turned away without waiting for the signal confirming Dave was dead. Only Boswell still watched.

This was now his operation. This was *his* death.

'OK, everybody! Make with the Yuletide glee!' Sawyer shouted, looking with shining eyes and his wide toothy smile at the diners, all of whom had risen in horror at the burst of firing. Slowly they sat down, but no one started eating again.

Into the room, hands on their heads, came the six survivors

119

of Boswell's little band, menaced by a Martlet's sub-machine gun. Behind him came Split, his gun in his right arm, blood soaking through his sleeve just below his left elbow. Traherne went straight across to him, tore apart his sleeve and began giving first-aid with a bottle of Scotch and a table-napkin to what appeared to be a mere flesh wound. Boswell liked that. A leader should take care of his men.

He resisted the urge to look again out of the window at that dark break in the snow where his own man lay.

Sawyer was clearly enjoying himself. He had torn a leg off a goose and was walking slowly round the table, chewing away with every expression of enjoyment. But Boswell noticed the perfect balance of the gun which lay apparently casually in the crook of his arm.

'This is one helluva rotten party,' said Sawyer. 'Hey, Boz, old boy, what ya gonna do to liven things up? These people will be wanting their money back if you don't start swinging. Won't they, honey?'

He leered down at Arabella, who met his gaze dispassionately. But clearly she lacked the power to disconcert Sawyer as she did Boswell.

'Well, Miss Allen. Arabella Allen, bless my soul. Arable Arabella. Man, I'd dearly love to plough that furrow. Eh, Boz, old chap?'

'Tarantyev!' hissed Traherne in protest. Round the table, several ears pricked with interest. Boswell started inwardly.

Tarantyev. The name he had been trying to recall earlier. The Soviet mad-boy whose brand of espionage involved assault, murder, arson—Boswell had always accepted the stories with considerable mental reservation, but now he began to wonder.

'Naughty, naughty,' reproved Sawyer. 'You know you shouldn't tell these good people who I am.'

'A slip,' said Traherne. 'But we have no time for this fooling.'

A slip. Boswell wondered. Traherne didn't seem the kind of man who would slip very easily. He sensed tension between these men. Again he tried to work out what motives could possibly exist for blowing such superb cover as T.T. and

T.T.H.M Now Traherne in his turn was making sure they knew who they were dealing with. Tit-for-tat? Not that Sawyer/Tarantyev seemed very bothered.

He was grinning amiably at Traherne. Then he turned to one of the others and spoke to him rapidly in a low voice. The man, the pale-faced drummer, nodded and went out. The odds were instantly improved. Traherne was still dressing Split's wound, which left only three men, armed and ready. But the nature of their weapons and, still more, the presence of so many women round the table made a break still too dangerous to consider.

Sawyer smiled sardonically at him, as though reading his thoughts, then crossed over to the window, opened it and shouted something to the drummer who had appeared out of the front door into the snow. The man waved in acknowledgment, then headed towards the barn in which the group's Bedford van was parked. Surely he wasn't going to start it! wondered Boswell. It would hardly be possible to get it out of the barn, let alone make an escape in it!

Sawyer was prowling round the table again. Traherne, his work on Split's arm finished, watched him blank-faced.

'Ladies, gentlemen,' said Sawyer. 'Many of you may be wondering just what the hell's going on here. Well, while we're waiting, I'm going to tell you. You have been deceived; yes, sir; you have been cheated. Let me introduce a few of your fellow-guests. Their official titles would mean very little to you, but if I tell you they are their countries' top spy-masters that'll make the picture clearer. Left to right then. Algernon Swinburne, British Security; Jules Leclerc, S.D.E.C.E., take a bow, Julie; Carlo Brucciani, of the Italian Uffizio; Willem Winterman of the Netherlands, sounds and smells like a cigar; Udo Himmelstor, of the Deutsche BND; where else? You've gotta give it to the Almighty; when it come to Germany, he did it all by type-casting. Eh, Udo, boy? Give us *Stille Nacht* again, you lousy crypto-Nazi you.'

It was said without much heat. In fact the whole speech lacked any real edge of anti-Western fanaticism. It appeared to Boswell to be merely a time-spinner. But if it lacked heat itself, it certainly generated it. Frau Himmelstor rose majestically to her feet and began to speak in German. Boswell was a fluent linguist and felt slightly shocked at some of the general reflections being offered on Sawyer's character and background. But it was a moving demonstration of loyalty to her husband. It was clear why the Valkyrie myth had such a hold on the Germanic imagination.

Sawyer obviously understood German also. He listened in silence for a few moments, then came round the table, snarling back in her own language in terms even more colloquially obscene. When he reached her he thrust her roughly back into her seat, still talking.

Then it happened. Herr Bear, inflamed by this attack, verbal and physical, on his wife, jumped to his feet, protesting noisily. Sawyer turned. Absurdly the German was attempting to draw the sword which went with the dress uniform. He got it halfway from his scabbard, then it stuck.

Sawyer threw back his head and laughed. Himmelstor, purple with fury, spat in his face and flung himself at him like a maddened buffalo. The sheer force of the attack took Sawyer by surprise and he was forced back on to the table. But with the instinctive reactions of the highly trained fighter his knee came up hard into Himmelstor's groin. And again. The German screamed, high and long. Sawyer forced his bulk back from him. For a second Boswell thought Sawyer was going to shoot him. Then he thrust the barrel of his gun savagely into the German's face, twice, three times, audibly smashing teeth and nose with the blows. Frau Cow screamed now. Sawyer brought the butt of the gun round in a final vicious blow which opened up the side of the German's face and the man's great bulk, flaccid now, nerveless, subsided to the floor, only a faint gurgling from the throat and a pink bubble, which kept on bursting and re-forming on his lips, showing he was alive.

Her face twisted with hatred, Frau Cow now flung herself at Sawyer's back and he turned to deal with her. Boswell was certain he would just as readily be just as violent with the woman, but other things began to happen.

Everyone's attention, including the armed men's, was on the fight. Except for Arabella's.

122

In one fluid movement she rose and hurled a bowlful of still steaming soup in the nearest Martlet's face. He staggered back screaming. If this had been the signal for a general assault on their captors, the gunmen would have been overpowered in a few seconds. But Boswell saw in a single glance there was no chance of this.

His own men were still standing by the wall, very closely covered. Those of the guests who might have done something had first to disentangle themselves from their womenfolk. And Boswell himself was at the wrong side of the table for attack.

But the right side, he realised instantly, for retreat. He rolled backwards out of his chair towards the window conveniently left open by Sawyer. There was no chance, he realised, as without pause he launched himself at the sill. Traherne had seized Split's gun and brought it to bear. Any doubts he might have had about the man's reluctance to shoot the innocent certainly did not extend to himself.

Then between his eyes and the menacing barrel rose an apparition. Arabella, her gown ballooning like a parachute, came bounding over the table to join him. A moment of agony followed, lasting only the split second it took for his impetus to carry him through the window, but seeming aeons longer. But the gun was silent. And his body, instantly rising from the ground, was crushed breathless and shaken back into the snow as Arabella landed on top of him.

13

*Where are they? Tell me when to fire. Where
are they—where are they?*

MR. NATHANIEL WINKLE

There was no time for gallantry. He pushed Arabella away
with great force and got to his feet once more.

Thank God it had been Traherne not Sawyer! he thought.
He'd have shot his own mother if she'd got in the way. And
he'd be at this very window within seconds.

Seizing Arabella's hand, he dragged her upright and set off
at a sprint towards the barn. For a second she resisted, clearly
(and reasonably) feeling they would be better off getting round
the side of the house out of the field of fire offered by the window. But equally clearly she acknowledged this was no time
for debate and, gathering up her skirts, she matched him stride
for stride.

Rapidly the snow deepened and began to catch their feet.
Boswell remembered the agonising slow motion of Dave's last
few strides. Then they were on the path his fatal run had
broken. Boswell pushed the girl in front of him to take advantage of the flattened snow. Any second now he expected
to hear the chatter of automatic fire behind them. Perhaps not
hear it. Perhaps the red-hot bullets would burn their way

through his clothes and flesh before their sound could travel to him from the house.

As they reached Dave's body, he risked a glance back. Framed in the window was Sawyer. It was too quick a glance to give more than the most general impression. Yet for ever afterwards a picture remained imprinted in his memory, ready for instant recall, of the man's face, twisted with fury and yet at the same time alive with tremendous pleasure and excitement, as he brought the sub-machine gun to bear.

'Down!' he screamed, thrusting at Arabella's back with all his might. She hardly needed the extra encouragement, but flung herself in a racing dive under the snow-covered protection of the tractor, turning instantly to drag Boswell after her as his own dive left him short. Behind him the snow flurried in a miniature blizzard as the Sterling began its excited chatter.

'What the hell did we have to come this way for?' demanded Arabella irately. 'There's far more cover round the back.'

'You got a gun?' enquired Boswell.

'No,' she said, surprised. 'You?'

'No, but I soon will have.'

He looked towards the little huddle of clothes and cold flesh that had been Dave.

'Of course!' She was quick. But no compliments.

'For Godsake, get it!'

He pictured once again the scene as Dave fell, arms flung out, gun slowly spinning forward to be swallowed up by the snow.

Sawyer had disappeared from the window, probably confident he could spare a moment to ensure that order was fully restored in the dining room. If they remained unarmed he could afford forever in this snow. Not only did it make speed impossible and escape to the village a long, fatiguing and dangerous job, but it also provided an undisguisable trail.

They needed that gun badly. Pushing first his arm, then the whole of his upper body beneath the snow, Boswell cast around for the weapon. For a moment he thought he had got it first go. Cold metal burned against his hand. He grunted in disappointment, choking in a mouthful of snow as he did so. It was only the hook at the end of the length of chain by which the tractor hauled the trees down from the hillside.

It took two more plunges before he found the gun.

When he surfaced from the snow he found Arabella making snowballs.

'What the hell!' he expostulated.

'Are you going to let me have the gun?' she asked.

'Certainly not!'

'Then I'll make the most of what I've got!'

'Don't be stupid!' he snapped. 'You start making tracks for the village. I'll take care of things here. Go on. Move!'

'And get myself shot? We've got company.'

From the house, with only minimal caution, emerged one of the Martlets. Boswell thought he recognised him as the red-haired bass guitarist. There was something about the way he carried his gun.

He stopped about forty feet from the barn.

'Mr. Boswell,' he called. 'Please come out and return to the house.'

'They're all very polite anyway,' murmured Arabella. 'Do we accept his invitation?'

'Not if you want to write your Christmas thank-you letters. Look at the window there.'

Dimly visible in the bay was a dark figure.

'Sawyer?'

'That's right. Fairly itching to let loose with that little toy of his again, I shouldn't be surprised.'

She looked thoughtful, then nodded.

'You could be right. He doesn't seem quite sound in the head somehow. What's he hope to achieve by all this?

'God knows, but I'm going to be around to find out. Come on, let's move.'

He began to wriggle away round the side of the barn. The girl looked at him curiously.

'Why don't you shoot him?' she gestured with a flick of her head towards the man standing before the house.

'Two reasons. First, I'm a rotten shot and that thing he's got pumps bullets out a damn' sight faster than this pop-gun.

126

Second, I don't really want to. He's done me no harm and he plays a fair guitar. Come on. Once we've got the barn between us and the house, we can make a run for it.'

It wasn't as simple as that. They made it round the back of the barn easily enough and Boswell was just about to make a dash for the line of trees, which like a child's painting seemed to lie flat and black, against the snow, when a sudden flurry of flakes on to his head made him look up. For a second he thought the blizzard must be returning. Then he saw above him the stiffly opening door of the hayloft. Next second, the pale drummer emerged.

Damning himself for a fool for forgetting the man was in the barn, Boswell flung himself against the side of the building; his feet went from under him and he crashed to the ground with a force even the blanket of snow couldn't muffle. Memories of John Wayne drawing, shooting, and killing two or three men as he fell off his horse, filled his mind. It plainly required a special gift. He was quite unable to find a way of pointing his gun, no matter how vaguely, in the right direction. Perhaps *up* presented special problems.

Fortunately *down* too presented its own difficulties, and the drummer looked most uncomfortable as he attempted to aim his sub-machine gun without falling out of the barn. But Boswell had little doubt who would succeed first. He was already trying to form his spread-eagled limbs into a hieroglyph of surrender when the drummer's head jerked back and a new whiteness erupted on his natural pallor.

Arabella, more primitively armed than either of the men, but firmly braced on her own two feet, had joined the fray. The second snowball was just as accurately aimed as the first, taking the drummer full in the mouth. Boswell shuddered as he thought of the cannonball-like consistency the snow had achieved under the shaping pressure of the girl's hands.

Above him, the drummer tottered crazily on the brink of the loft door. For a moment it seemed impossible he would not crash down on top of them. Then with a gargantuan effort, using the weight of the machine gun like a wire-walker's pole, he managed to pull himself back from the edge. But he had overcompensated and a third snowball, catching him a

127

glancing blow on the shoulder, was enough to send him top-
pling backwards into the barn.

'Come on!' said Arabella, pulling Boswell to his feet. 'For
Godsake, when are you going to start using that gun?'

'You're not so hot yourself,' he grunted. 'You almost
missed with your third shot.'

But clearly the time had come to take her advice. The bass-
guitarist, attracted by the noise behind the barn, had moved
in a wide circle to his left and suddenly came into view. Boswell aimed the automatic and squeezed the trigger. The gun
barked most satisfactorily in the snow-silence and the guitarist, shocked to find himself so unexpectedly under fire, set off
at a scrambling sliding gallop to find cover.

Putting another shot up into the hayloft just to discourage
any activity there, Boswell hurried after Arabella, who had
already started on a painfully slow-motion run towards the
trees.

It seemed to last for ever. It wasn't thoughts of John Wayne
that filled his mind now, but of all those—cowboys, Indians,
soldiers, civilians—who had ever run in terror, knowing that
any moment might bring burning metal to quench its heat in
the fragile flesh.

As he plunged headlong behind the solid comfort of the
nearest tree, he heard a gun start up, whether from the hayloft or the house he did not know. Nor care to find out. There
was a series of solid, chunky noises—like tent-pegs being ham-
mered into hard ground—and something whipped across his
forehead, leaving a thin, bloody trail for his finger to trace.

He looked at the blood in disbelieving wonderment. The
reality of being hit was strangely different from the fear of it,
but no less a burden to the mind.

'Boz!' hissed Arabella from somewhere much deeper in the
trees.

Bravely he turned towards her and smiled so that the sight
of his wound should not be too great a shock.

'For Godsake, stop lying there! Another burst like that will
chop that blasted tree down!'

There was no trace of sympathy in her tone. He crawled

128

towards her through the snow which became thinner and patchier as he got deeper into the copse.

'OK?' she asked.

'Yes. Just a scratch,' he murmured.

'I saw. A splinter. By God, those choppers they've got certainly make the wood fly! Do you reckon they'll come after us?'

'How the hell should I know?'

She looked surprised.

'Well, you're the big secret agent expert, aren't you? Me, I'm just a plain working girl on holiday.'

More than that. Much more than that, he thought, looking at her.

He began to smile. She returned first his gaze, then his smile. The smiles broadened into grins, then broke out into loud and only distantly hysterical laughter.

'What're you laughing at?' she gasped.

'You! I mean, us. What an extraordinary pair . . . to be . . . doing this!'

Indeed they were. Arabella's beautiful satin gown was ruined, but she still looked very much the early Victorian maiden. Her exertions had dragged her *décolletage* even lower than it was originally, and her exquisitely rounded shoulders and breasts were very exposed to the elements. She was pure Pre-Raphaelite Ophelia, were it not for the strength of the chin and the deep gold suntan of all the exposed skin.

Boswell stopped laughing and pulled off his long-tailed jacket.

'Here,' he said. 'You'll freeze.'

He put it round her shoulders, ignoring her protests.

'They wore plenty of padding in their waistcoats then,' he said. 'Nice and warm. It gave the impression of being broad-chested.'

'So it's all a pretence,' she said with a smile.

'True. Not an accusation I could make of you,' he replied, glancing down at her bust.

'Thanks for the jacket,' she said ironically, wrapping it tightly round her. 'The cold will do you good.'

'The cold with kill us both if we don't keep moving.' he

answered, taking her hand and setting off more purposefully than he felt on a line roughly parallel to the long drive leading away from Dingley Dell.

'Will they come after us?'

'I don't know. One perhaps. Sawyer won't want to leave himself understaffed back there.'

She looked at him doubtfully.

'I don't know. Take away your men and there's precious little resistance there. Especially after the way he dealt with poor old Herr Bear.'

She shuddered, partly at the memory and partly at the cold, as a thin wind soughed its way through the branches above them, spilling snow on to their heads.

'What would you do if you were Sawyer? Or rather what did Traherne call him? Tarantyev?'

If I were Sawyer, he thought, I would . . . Well, first of all I'd damn' well know what I was trying to do! The Home Counties . . . Christmas Day . . . sub-machine guns . . . no escape route . . . what did it all add up to?

Precious little that made sense. Wardle staring up at him from under the green ice; Swinburne breathing shallowly like a puny kitten that can't make up its mind to live or to die; Himmelstor falling over the table, his face ripped open like a peeled blood orange.

And, most immediately important, Arabella and himself, ill-clothed and ill-equipped, being pursued like hares through the snow.

'If I were Sawyer,' he said aloud, 'I would give in gracefully. There's no way out for him.'

'You don't look like a graceful giver-in to me,' she answered.

'Neither does Sawyer. So we'll assume he's sent at least one man after us just to make sure we don't reach the village.'

The wisdom of this assumption became apparent a few minutes later. The copse thinned out and finally turned into a mere line of trees spaced at thirty-foot intervals. A parallel line some twenty feet away marked the other side of the road, though there was nothing about the unbroken surface of the snow to indicate this. This democratic effect of the snow, reducing bog and tarmac to apparent equality, was a matter of some concern. Boswell knew the land surrounding Dingley Dell pretty well, but this dramatic change of colour scheme, the more subtle shift in contouring, and the complete disappearance of some low hedgerows, all combined to make him hesitate about leaving the line of the drive.

Beside him Arabella was gently bobbing up and down on the balls of her feet. He didn't need to ask why. The thin shoes she was wearing must give even less protection than his own, and he knew how cold his feet felt. Once more he carefully scanned the terrain they had just covered. The real problem might after all turn out to be how to surrender without getting shot.

'How long do you reckon?' asked Arabella, her teeth chattering.

'Till what?'

'Till we get there.'

'The village?' God, she was an optimist! 'Perhaps a little longer than we thought.'

'To hell with the village!' She laughed derisively. 'Dressed like this, I've got as much chance of walking ten miles as of finding sixpence in my Christmas pudding. Less. No, the cottage will do me fine. We *are* making for the cottage, aren't we?'

The cottage. Of course! The old gate-cottage at the end of the drive. It was absurd. He must have seen it a hundred times, Arabella only once as she arrived the previous day. Yet its existence had faded completely from his mind.

True, it was sadly dilapidated now. But it would provide shelter, warmth. Perhaps more. He knew the gamekeepers (both his and the genuine ones) used the place for shelter and storage. There might be a shovel there, perhaps even a pair of gumboots.

'That's right,' he said easily. 'We'll use it as a base camp for our final assault. Come on.'

Masterfully taking her hand, he stepped out of the cover of the trees.

There was an instant chatter of gun-fire and snow spurted up some five or six yards away as the bullets ploughed into it. It was difficult to say who jerked who back under cover, but they lay in an undignified tangle for a moment, breathless, each feeling as if an arm had almost been wrenched from its socket.

'This is what you meant by the final assault, is it?' she whispered vehemently.

Boswell ignored her and released the safety-catch on his automatic. It was some small comfort to realise that his enemies, no matter how well in theory, were as inexpert in the field as he himself was proving. Sawyer, he felt certain, would have let them move another twenty yards out of the protection of the copse. Nor would he have let the odd perspective of the snow make him miscalculate his range.

He had no doubt their pursuer (Singular? There had only been one gun firing, certainly) would learn fast. He would just have to learn as well.

He turned to Arabella and began whispering.

'He must have reckoned on us following the drive. I place him on the other side about fifty, sixty yards back, so it's no contest if I try to take him on with this thing.'

'We could try snowballs again,' said Arabella.

'Shut up. Flight is always the better part of fight. We'll break off at right angles here. That'll keep the copse between us and the drive. There's a hedge about fifty yards over there, if I remember right. Once on the other side, it'll give us cover right down to the back of the cottage.'

He paused, half expecting dissent.

'What are we waiting for?' she asked.

Once out of the copse, the going was very tough. The snow was always a minimum of three feet deep and as they approached the ridge of whiteness which marked the line of the hedge, it grew deeper. Boswell led the way, using his arms like a 'butterfly' swimmer, until one downward stroke met with sudden thorny resistance. They had reached the hedge.

It was a good thick mixture of hawthorn and beech and it was plain impossible to force a way through. Boswell bent forward, braced his hands on his knees and grunted, 'Over you go.' Arabella vaulted on to his back, if not lightly at least with more agility than he felt capable of, scrambled up on to his shoulders and jumped gracefully over the hedge. There was a satisfying thump as she landed. Satisfying not just on the basis of personal malice, but because it confirmed his hope that the considerable drifting on this side meant there was relatively little snow on the lee-side.

His own traversing of the hedge was an undignified process and painful with it. The thump he made as Arabella finally dragged him free from the clinging hawthorn seemed even more solid. But he had been right. The ditch on this side was only scattered with snow, though a couple of feet further out, it was as thick as ever.

Arabella was picking up great armfuls of the stuff and tossing it over the hedge.

'What's that for?' he asked.

'A break in the snow-line along the hedge will stick out like a palm-tree in the desert,' she answered.

'True,' he said, 'but he'll spot our tracks anyway.'

'Not so easily. And I did my best to sweep the snow in over them as we came.'

'Did you now? Clever old you.'

He meant it. But he meant the irony too. It seemed desirable to establish firmly who was the leader of this expedition. No, that was absurd. Survival was all that mattered in their present circumstances. But the question of dominance in their relationship was clearly one which had to be resolved. Though perhaps the relationship would end with the circumstances which had caused it.

Perhaps all their relationships would end then if he didn't keep his mind on the job in hand. He crouched lower and increased his pace along the ditch.

They reached the ruined cottage without further incident. The door screeched nerve-rackingly on its warped hinges, but it was good to know that the entry of other visitors would be just as noisily announced.

It was a small place, one up, one down, with a kitchen. Dilapidated but not too dusty, as if someone felt it worth while to keep it tidy. This reminded Boswell of his hopes that the gamekeepers might have left some gear here for ease of access. He didn't have to look far. Indeed there wasn't far he could look. A large oak cupboard, which with a chair, a stool and a sadly listing table provided the total downstairs furnishing, opened to reveal a treasure-trove. A pair of wellingtons, a pair of ancient but serviceable leather boots, an ex-army groundsheet cape, and greatcoat. And a short-handled spade.

'Clever old you,' said Arabella in her turn. 'God, I'm freezing!'

It was only now they had stopped moving that Boswell realised how cold he was. The snow had melted and soaked its way through every inch of his clothing. But starting a fire was far too dangerous. The smoke would be spotted a mile off.

Arabella had disappeared, he realised. He heard her footsteps on the wooden stairs.

'Careful!' he called, concerned about the state of the woodwork generally.

A creak overhead told him she had reached the first floor and he set off after her, keeping as close to the wall as possible.

The bedroom still seemed to have its uses too. An old iron bedstead held pride of place there and, miracle of miracles, a couple of threadbare blankets were draped over it. A useful place for the keepers to snatch an hour's rest in the long watches of the night.

'Undo the hooks, will you?' said Arabella, turning her back to him.

He performed the task without really grasping her purpose, though briefly there crossed his mind the fluttering fancy that his masculine presence had driven her mad with desire. He was quickly disenchanted even as she stepped out of her dress.

'Modesty's not going to make me freeze to death,' she said. 'But one step in the wrong direction could be painful for you.'

'This looks like a step in the right direction,' he said admiringly, as the rest of her clothes fell to the ground and she began towelling her goose-pimpled body with one of the blankets.

It seemed like a good idea and quickly he followed suit. It was exhilarating to feel the blood begin to circulate once more

134

as he rubbed the rough cloth violently against his flesh, contorting himself in his efforts to reach the centre of his back.

'Swops,' said Arabella, who was having the same problem.

'Ahh!' he said, as she sent the warming strokes running up and down his spine.

'Your turn,' he said, and began the same process on her long, brown beautifully moulded back. It was a mistake, he knew instantly. Without help, he was not capable of this kind of restraint. Not even cold and wet with an armed man hunting for him outside. The slap in the face was what he needed to set things back on an even keel. So, let her slap.

Resigned to his fate, he took her shoulders and turned her slowly towards him. She looked up at him steadily, her gaze again holding his, which wanted to be running wildly over the hills and valleys of her body. Slowly still, he pulled her towards him. Still she did nothing. Their bodies met.

'It's just for the heat,' she said calmly. Then they kissed.

And downstairs the door screeched. Someone had just entered the cottage.

14

Then you are not dead! Oh, say you are not dead!

MISS RACHAEL

Arabella was not certain what she had intended next. Boswell, she was certain, had reached the point where he would be guided by her. If, without breaking off their kiss, she had wrapped the blankets round them and pulled him down with her on to the bed, there would have been no resistance. She herself was not far off that delicious dream state in which nothing exists outside one's own sensuality. But she still had choice.

Till the door screeched open below. Then there was no longer a choice.

She was pushed gently away by Boswell, who knelt quietly down beside his discarded clothing. She admired the long, lean length of his body and retrospectively decided what she would have done. Now his movements became less certain, however, and she knelt beside him.

'What?' she mouthed.

'The gun. Where?' He looked desperately around once more, then squatted on his haunches in complete dejection.

'When I came over the hedge, I must have . . . I'm sorry,' he whispered.

Arabella shook her head at him and strained her ears. There it was again, unmistakable. a foot placed softly, furtively, on the stairs.

Boswell heard it too and stood up, moving protectively between her and the door. It was amazing how a little bit of sex could bring out the old chivalrous hangover in some men. Very touching really, but hardly helpful in their present circumstances.

The window offered nothing. It was small, square and looked unopenable. In any case, nudity was far from being the best state for running through the snow.

She remembered one of her Uncle Sam's maxims when he used to take her on hunting trips in South Africa.

Every disadvantage must be someone's advantage. It can be yours if you only look at it right.

It made sense. What he said usually did. Swiftly she gesticulated at Boswell to position himself behind the door. He did so, reluctantly, obviously feeling that the dangers of a sub-machine gun being fired indiscriminately in such a small place were far too great. He was right. Unless the bearer of the gun was too distracted to get a shot in.

The stairs creaked again. She flung a blanket on the bed and stretched her magnificent body on it full length. Boswell stared at her in amazement. She winked at him, then closed her eyes. A faint smile played on her lips.

Now he saw her plan. A tethered goat. Distraction for the predator. It could work. Christ, it was certainly distracting *him*!

The door creaked open. Arabella forced herself to breathe deeply, rhythmically, as though in a sound sleep. She sensed the amazed eyes on her, heard the intaken breath, the two hesitant steps forward. Boswell must be poised for attack. She sighed deeply and rolled over on her side to create maximum attention—holding effect. Still no sound of violent movement. Only another couple of paces forward. She had a sense now of the man standing poised over her, staring down, lust growing in his gut as his eyes caressed the flesh offered up so freely to him. Perhaps Boswell had . . . had what? Fainted?

For Godsake! A finger touched her gently, almost reluctantly, on the shoulder. She opened her eyes.

Above her hung a leonine face, a ginger mane like a sunburst framing a pair of bright blue but very puzzled eyes. She opened her mouth to scream.

'Hello, Jimmy,' said Boswell pleasantly.

The man spun round in alarm, looked even more surprised at finding a naked man than a naked woman. Then his body relaxed and a yellow-toothed smile broke out beneath his tangled beard.

'Good day to you, Mr. Boswell,' he said, touching the brim of the old straw hat he wore, a gesture more derisive than servile. 'Sorry to interrupt, I'm sure. Very sorry, madam.'

He leered complacently down at Arabella.

'Thought Santa Claus had brought me what I wanted at last,' he chortled. 'Without the wrapping.'

'What are you going here, Jimmy?' asked Boswell.

'Needn't ask you that, eh, sir?' said Jimmy. Arabella climbed off the bed and wrapped a blanket round her. The veiling of her charms seemed to be enough to switch off the old man's lecherous familiarity.

'Not doing any harm,' he said. 'Thought I'd try my luck up at the Dell last night, it being Christmas Eve. But the snow was coming down so thick, when I reached here, I thought I'd better stick. I was round the back when you must have come.

'Just greed,' he added philosophically to Arabella. 'I got myself given a nice pheasant and a couple of rabbits yesterday, by a Yankee gent, so I was comfortably fixed. But I flogged 'em in the village and thought I'd get me Christmas dinner in the kitchen at the Dell.'

'A Yankee gent?' asked Boswell, glancing at Arabella.

'That's right. Nice chap. Found him in the old waiting room at the station—that's one of my spots now they don't use it no more—sprucing himself up a bit, he were. I thought he was going to turn nasty at first, but he changed his tune in the end when he saw I meant no harm. Went off on one of your coaches, Mr. Boswell.'

You don't know how lucky you were, thought Boswell.

Tarantyev must have very seriously considered killing the old tramp. But this confirmed it was that Russian who had shot the man on the hillside also. It had been a puzzle that he had apparently arrived on the afternoon train.

'Any chance of a bite to eat at the Dell, it being Christmas Day and all?' said Jimmy, bent on making the most of the situation, even to the extent of a mild hint of blackmail. 'Can I say you sent me, Mr. Boswell?'

'I doubt if it would do you much good at the moment.'

Boswell shivered and Arabella handed him the other blanket. He started slightly, as though just noticing his own nakedness, and grinned ruefully at her.

'Can you hang on downstairs a moment, Jimmy?' he said. Obligingly the tramp left, after a series of knowing nods and winks.

'Who is *that*?' demanded Arabella.

'A local gent of the road,' said Boswell. 'Harmless enough. He could be useful.'

'For what?'

'For getting to the village. If anyone can make it, he can. Sawyer's boy is after *us*, isn't he? Almost certainly once he lost us, he'll have covered the route to the village. If we let ourselves be seen—distantly and safely, of course—we can draw him away and leave the road clear for Jimmy to get through.'

Arabella was doubtful.

'Can we trust him?'

Boswell laughed.

'If you mean, is he likely to turn out to be a lieutenant-general in the KGB, the answer's an emphatic "no"!'

'Nice to be so certain,' murmured Arabella. 'OK. But is he reliable to deliver a message to someone who will help?'

'I think so. Jimmy's well known to the village bobby. Harmless and sometimes helpful.'

'Which?'

'Both, I suppose,' grinned Boswell. 'But bright enough to take notice.'

Arabella was no longer listening. Her attention was centred on the door.

139

'Funny,' she whispered. 'I didn't hear the stairs creak as he went down.'

Boswell whipped the door open in one smooth movement. Grinning unrepentantly, Jimmy stepped back inside.

'I should have known,' said Boswell. 'Right, Jim lad. You heard. We're in a spot of bother. Will you carry a message to the village?'

'I could do, Mr. Boswell. If I was going that way.'

'And what other way would you be going?'

'To the Dell. For my dinner.'

Arabella rolled her eyes in exasperation.

'The old fool!' she muttered.

Boswell calmed her with an amused glance.

'Don't you recognise bargaining when you hear it? All right, Jimmy. Sunday dinner in the kitchen at Dingley Dell for the next six months?'

'Done!' said the old tramp happily. He got another month out of Boswell on the strength of an old pencil-stub he produced, this being the only writing implement they had between them. And he threw in a piece of advice gratis when he saw Boswell glumly contemplating putting on his damp clothes once more.

'Tear up the blankets,' he said, nodding with enthusiasm for his own expertise. 'Tie the strips round your limbs. Best thing out for keeping you warm!'

Arabella would have preferred a large Scotch and a red-hot bath, but she had to agree there was something in the old man's advice when she tried it—after he had withdrawn from the room even more reluctantly than before.

Downstairs they divided their booty, while Jimmy watched with bright eyes, inwardly ruminating on his own past refusal to take anything from the cottage on the grounds of preserving it as a safe resting place. Clearly his scruples were not shared by all.

Arabella got the wellingtons (which were slightly smaller than the boots) and the groundsheet. Boswell wore the rest.

'Right, Jimmy,' he said. 'Give us ten minutes or so before you set out. Be sure of that, eh? How long do you reckon it will take you?'

'Long time, if I can do it at all,' said Jimmy. 'The lane's likely filled with snow like a hole in the ground.'

'You'd better take the shovel,' said Boswell, chucking him the implement.

'Ta,' said Jimmy, delighted to be going away with something—especially something legitimately given in the presence of a witness. Nothing had been said about returning it.

Boswell felt some qualms as he and Arabella slipped out once more into the snow.

'I hope he's all right,' he said.

'Why?' asked the girl surprised. 'What's worrying you?'

'If this didn't work,' said Boswell carefully, 'if someone decided to shoot old Jimmy just to be on the safe side, well, it would be my fault. For involving him, I mean.'

'You're the funniest spy I've ever met,' she answered.

'You've met a few, then?' he asked casually.

She wagged an admonishing finger at him.

'Still not trusting your faithful companion, are you? Lead on, Lone Ranger. Tonto will bring up the rear.'

'Hi-yo, Silver,' he said. Suddenly the clouds above parted and a wintry sun spilt pale light through the chasm on to the wooded ridge which rose sharply to the right of Dingley Dell and ran away more gently south towards the snow-hidden line of the road. Arabella felt strangely excited, as if they were setting out on some perilous but inevitably safe-ending quest at the completion of which all the bonhommie, piety and honest, sentimental merriment of the Dickensian Christmas-myth would be waiting for them. Beside this vision the self-indulgent play-acting of Dingley Dell Enterprises Ltd. seemed tawdry, *kitsch*, almost offensive. She could laugh at herself, as she had laughed during her African trip when, alone by her camp-fire in the evening, Rider Haggard notions of her journey had thronged in on her. But the laughter did not dispel, rather was absorbed into, the imaginings.

Boswell was looking at her quizzically, affectionately.

'Come on,' he said. 'We'll head up the ridge. We'll stick to cover till we're three-quarters of the way up, then show ourselves. If he's down there by the road, he's bound to see us moving against the snow.'

'So he is. Him with his little pop-gun. And us with our snowballs.'

He shrugged.

'I said I was sorry about losing it. Still perhaps we're better off without it. It's no use against those choppers, and I might have shot Jimmy the second he stepped through the door. We're better off with our sticks.'

Both of them had helped themselves to a four-foot-long oaken-stave, formerly part of the fencing which had once surrounded the cottage. If nothing else, they would be useful for probing the depth of the snow as they made their way over the frequently uneven terrain.

Cautiously they set off, moving back along the line of the drive again to start with, using the colonnade of trees as cover. The snow was never less than knee deep, but the old tramp's advice on lagging their legs at the top of their boots seemed to work and their feet remained dry. It was hard work, however, and even harder once they left the flat drive to follow a line of rhododendron bushes which ran obliquely up the rising terrain towards the distant ridge. The dark glossy green of the bushes' leaves showed triumphantly through and beneath the snow which weighed them down. It was like an earnest of survival. A robin appeared from the middle of one bush to investigate them and piped querulously in their direction. Arabella wished she had had a biscuit or anything edible to give it. The thought of food made her recall her own interrupted dinner. All that superb goose must now be lying neglected and cold, Not that there was anything wrong with cold goose. Indeed no. A cottage loaf, freshly buttered. A mound of stuffing. A glass of beer. And a leg of goose in her hand before a roaring fire.

She was awoken from her reverie by a sharp poke from Boswell's stick. Her mental wanderings had been accompanied by physical wanderings and she was up to her breast in snow. Exploration with her own stick revealed that she was in some kind of hollow and another couple of steps would have brought the level up to her head.

They were both damp now, but it was dampness from the sweat of exertion rather than snow. They had both almost forgotten their diversionary function and merely reaching the crest of the ridge had become end enough in itself. It seemed to get no nearer and Arabella began to doubt very seriously whether she could make it.

Then Boswell stopped and pointed down the slope.

'Look,' he said.

From the double row of hedge-tops which marked the line of the road, a solitary figure was floundering through the snow towards them. It was obviously very deep down there. But if there had been any doubts about who it was, they would have been dispelled by the weapon he held one-handed above his head for protection, like a man wading across a river.

'It's worked,' said Arabella.

'I hope so. Though if Jimmy makes as poor time as we've been doing, it's hardly worth while.'

Boswell was, in fact, more than a little concerned that no attempts whatsoever seemed to have been made to contact the hotel. He knew he was right to act as if it wouldn't be. Escape had been instinctive. In fact, after Arabella's efforts in the dining room, not to escape would have seemed most unchivalrous. But secretly he had felt that his efforts would be swiftly negatived by the arrival of an investigatory team sent by headquarters who must be concerned at the breaking of contact with Dingley Dell. Sure, it was Christmas Day. And of course it would take time to organise a snow-plough and men. But the blizzard has been finished for two hours at least. Even a helicopter flight was possible, though the snow would make landing difficult.

But something *must* be happening. If it wasn't, if British Security this holy afternoon was being served by sleeping the sleep of the gluttonous through Her Majesty's tele-speech, then Jimmy became very important. And he had rather less trust in the old tramp than he had implied to Arabella.

Below, the pursuer seemed to have got himself out of the deepest of the snow and was now moving comparatively swiftly in a series of zig-zags, using his gun as a prop and a depth-tester. He was within range, but it would have been a very difficult shot, uphill and in the snow. Now and then he stopped and seemed to be looking speculatively up at them.

'He thinks we've still got a gun,' said Boswell. 'He'll get as near as he thinks he can safely. Then he'll start blazing away.'

'I propose we don't wait for that,' said Arabella seriously.

'Carried *nem. con.*,' answered Boswell.

They resumed their climb and held their own, perhaps even gained a few yards on their pursuer whom Boswell had identified as the bass guitarist.

'He's in no hurry,' said Arabella.

'Why should he be? We're not going anywhere that bothers him. In fact we're getting nearer to the house all the time.'

They were almost at the top of the ridge now. A few more yards would see them in the trees. Boswell glanced back. The bass guitarist had stopped and was kneeling in the snow. He must have decided that he couldn't let them reach shelter without making some kind of effort. It was a decision perhaps not too far removed in feeling from Boswell's own act of escape.

'Oh look!' Arabella called.

Ahead of them, startled by their approach, a hare sat up in the snow, long ears twitching. Boswell moved his feet and the noise made up its mind for it. With an athletic bound, it took off down the hillside in a flurry of white, disappearing completely sometimes as it landed, then reappearing, comically, beautifully, in a series of tremendous leaps. It swept round in a wide arc which took it close to the guitarist who abandoned his preparation to shoot in favour of watching the beast.

Finally it disappeared from sight. The man turned and looked up the slope. Then awkwardly, rather shyly, he made a small movement of the gun and resumed his climb without firing.

Boswell lifted his hand to shoulder height and turned to Arabella.

'What was all that about?' she asked.

'I think he'd rather be enjoying his post-Christmas-pud indigestion too. Come on before he changes his mind.'

Under the trees the snow was much thinner. Quickly they made their way across the ridge till they found themselves once more looking down on Dingley Dell, a little higher than their walk the previous day had taken them.

'What now?' asked Arabella.

'I don't know,' admitted Boswell. 'I just wish to hell I knew what was going on, that's all.'

'There's only one way to find out. Let's get back into the house!'

He looked at her in amazement.

'You're joking!'

'You try me! Not by the front door, you fool. Through the back kitchen, perhaps. Or a window. What do you want to do? Wait here for Segovia to catch up with us, and go back inside at the end of a gun? Or in a wheelbarrow? Come on, Boz! Let's have some constructive thinking.'

So saying, she marched indignantly away down the slope.

'Arabella!' yelled Boswell. 'Hold on!'

She ignored him, and strode on.

'Watch out, Arabella!'

She cast a scornful smile over her shoulder and took another step.

Her smile didn't even have time to become surprise before she disappeared completely from sight.

Horrified, Boswell rushed forward, slowing as he neared the point of disappearance. It would do no good if he too went over the edge. It was, of course, the small quarry they had examined the day before. The snow had drifted into it to such an extent that the edge had completely disappeared and the bank of snow did not begin to slope away for another yard and a half.

Cautiously he peered down. For a moment he feared complete disaster. Then the smooth surface of the snow drift began to be disturbed about twelve feet below. First a hand came out, then an arm. Finally with an eruption like a white volcano, Arabella's head and shoulders broke the surface. She stood there, gasping and spluttering, as she wiped the snow from her face.

'Are you OK?' hissed Boswell.

She looked up at him with an expression of fury and indignation which was its own answer. Boswell's next words did nothing to disperse it.

'Lie down!' he whispered hoarsely.

145

'What!' she cried.

'Sshh! Lie down. Play wounded!'

Understanding dawned. She was to play the staked goat again. It had worked once, in a kind of way. It might work this time. She stretched herself out at full length in the snow, twisting her limbs awkwardly. Naked on an iron bedstead had been bad, but this was far worse. Opening one eye, she looked up for sympathy. Boswell was nowhere in sight. She closed her eye again.

The bass guitarist came cautiously through the trees. He was cold and wet and rather bewildered. He had been trained for this kind of work, true. But that had been nearly ten years earlier. Back in the Centre, his controller had already then conceived the idea of using this new, decadent, English pop-cult as a cover for operations. It was fluid, kaleidoscopic, idiosyncratic, permissive; yet at the same time respectable, even reverable, international. Traherne had been the first. Slowly the group had been built around him. Its composition sometimes changed; sometimes one or more of the members had been legitimate. But for the past three years they had all been operatives.

They had done their work well. *All* their work. He had enjoyed it all. They had been in the charts. Even appeared on television. God, how that must have made them laugh back home! Five Soviet agents, long-haired, sexual, singing about the need to forget politics and love everybody! It had been fun.

But now it was all done. All finished. At best they might get back to the USSR, perhaps even be kissed on the cheeks by someone important, given a medal. But there weren't many openings in Moscow for a twenty-eight-year-old pop bass guitarist who had half forgotten his native language.

He stopped at the edge of the trees and cautiously surveyed the scene before him. No sign of movement, but tracks, broad deep tracks through the snow for about ten yards. Then they seemed to stop.

Carefully he moved forward. The roof of the house was in sight. It was warm in there. On the other hand, Tarantyev, the madman, was in there. Perhaps it was better to be outside after all.

He reached the place where the tracks ended and saw why. The ground fell away sharply here. He peered down and drew in his breath in a sharp hiss, at the same time bringing his gun up to the 'ready' position. Below, lying twisted on her side, was the girl. His stomach churned at the sight. He had had no desire to shoot anybody, certainly not a girl. But he must be at least partly to blame that she was lying so twisted and still down there.

Ten years was a long time. Immediately after his training ten years earlier, he would never have forgotten the man.

Boswell burst out of the snow beneath which he had buried himself and hurled himself at the guitarist's back. Had the attack taken place on level ground, the element of surprise would have been completely triumphant. But the force of his rush proved disastrous.

The guitarist half turned, tried to bring his gun round. Boswell's outstretched hands took him round the throat. He was hurled backwards and, locked together, the two men plunged out of sight into the snowdrift. It was nightmarish down there. The guitarist had lost his gun but managed instinctively to get a grip on Boswell. Neither man dared release his hold on the other. It was a question of company as much as contention. To be alone beneath that cold, powdery, flaky, clinging greyness was unthinkable. They rolled over, flinging token blows at each other. For a second Boswell managed to free himself and stand up, his head appearing through the snow a couple of yards from Arabella who looked at him, half amazed, half amused. Then his feet were swept from under him and he submerged once more.

Finally, locked in each others arms like passionate lovers, the two men rolled together out of the drift, only letting go of each other and rising to their feet when they realised they were back in the open air.

They faced each other warily, both puffing and panting from their exertions. A light steam drifted up from their bodies, so violent had their recent activity been. The guitarist's face drifted to Arabella and registered betrayal when he saw

147

her standing there uninjured. She felt oddly uncomfortable.

'Hold it,' she said, as the men began making tentative movements towards each other. They stopped.

'Look,' she said to the guitarist. 'It's two to one. I'm not just going to stand by and watch like a helpless damsel, you realise. The minute I get a chance, I'm going to beat your head in. Why not sit down and talk things over?'

The guitarist cast an ironic look at the snow ground.

'Lady,' he said, 'you talk sense. Just remember, it's guns that count and all the guns down there belong to us. So it's you who's outnumbered. Why don't we all stroll down together and get out of these wet things?'

He had a pleasant flat North London accent. He smiled as he spoke, but he didn't really seem happy.

'No, thanks,' said Boswell. 'There's a man called Tarantyev down there and I think he'd shoot us just for kicks.'

The guitarist looked even unhappier.

'No. No,' he said uncertainly. He took a step towards Arabella and stretched out his hands pleadingly.

'No one need get hurt,' he said. 'Believe me.'

'Oh, I do,' she began, quite moved. Then one of the pleading hands grabbed her forearm, she felt herself spun round and hurled bodily towards Boswell. He seemed uncertain whether catching her or avoiding her was the best thing in the circumstances and the result, as so often in cases of hesitation, was collapse. The guitarist meanwhile had dived back into the snowdrift and was already surfacing with the sub-machine gun in his hands. Boswell tried to push the girl from athwart his body, but without much success. Arabella, very winded, had just enough strength to raise her head and look at the guitarist, wondering if he would fire. It needed a *deus ex machina* to save them now.

On cue, the machine arrived. A distant muttering became a threshing roar and down from the greyness above stooped a silver and white helicopter.

It moved twice round the house, finally hovering low over the area between the barn and the frontage. The draught from its rotors beat the snow below into a whirlwinding fury as frightening as the blizzard the night before. It took a few seconds for Boswell to see that this was purposeful, a deliberate clearing of an area to make a safe landing.

So his confidence in the efficiency of HQ, even on Christmas Day, had been right. He only hoped to God they could handle the situation down there. There could still be a disaster. Whatever else they expected, it would hardly amount to five men with sub-machine guns.

The helicopter landed, the hatch slid open, two armed men leapt out and to his horror ran straight towards the house. He rose to shout at them, not that there was any hope of his voice being heard above the slackening note of the 'copter's engine, but Arabella held on to his arm and, looking back, he saw the guitarist, gun held very steadily, shaking his head.

When he looked back the men had disappeared into the house. There was a long pause. Then a short burst of automatic fire. He felt sick to his heart. It didn't seem likely that the gunfire could mean anything except disaster for the newcomers. Unless those held captive inside had taken a hand. There were experts enough present after all.

The front door of the house burst open. Out into the snow sprinted a man. Only death at your back moved a man like that, thought Boswell, remembering his own panic as he ran for cover behind the barn. From inside the house came a vicious, prolonged burst of fire. The running man was caught in the shoulder so that he spun round to face the house. His chest bubbled in a cauldron of red, visible even from Boswell's distance. The firing stopped and the lifeless figure subsided on his back into the snow.

The shock of the scene was scarcely alleviated by his recognition of the dead man. It was the pale drummer. The new arrivals must be in control. But the violence they had just seen enacted before them had nothing to do with good and bad, right and wrong.

The guitarist was shaking all over as he moved forward to look down the hill at the body. He made no effort at resistance as Boswell took the gun fom him.

'It's Johnny. They killed Johnny,' was all he could say.

'Come on,' said Boswell, putting his arm round him to give support. 'Let's go down now.'

149

Carefully they made their way down the hill. The guitarist wanted to go over to his friend's body, but Boswell prevented him. There would be time enough later when strangers had disguised some of the obscene horror.

The centre of activities in Dingley Dell seemed to have moved from the dining room to the parlour. One of the rescue team, a yellow-haired broken-nosed man not known to Boswell, stepped out to meet them, gun levelled.

'It's all right,' said Boswell wearily. 'I'm Boswell.'

Without answering the man took the machine gun away from him. A wise precaution till you were absolutely sure, thought Boswell.

At the bottom of the stairs another of the Martlets lay dead. Through the open door of the parlour he could see Traherne standing, hands clasped on his head, face expressionless. He should have felt triumphant, but somehow instead he felt empty, desolate.

The yellow-haired man waved them through the door with his gun. Gently he pushed the guitarist before him. What happened next was a complete shock. The guitarist stopped in the doorway. His slack, lifeless pose vanished, it was like a marionette when someone tautens the strings; he became upright, rigid. Then with an unintelligible cry, savage with fury, he jumped forward into the room. Immediately there was a shot, just one, but close enough to fling the man back into Boswell's arms, blood oozing from his chest.

'You stupid . . . what the hell . . . who?' cried Boswell in an agony of protest. The door swung fully open now. Next to Traherne he saw the other Martlet, Split. Then Leclerc, Brucciani, Swinburne, Winterman, all the delegates, all with their hands clasped docilely on their heads.

'Be welcome to Dingley Dell, Mr. Boswell!' boomed out a familiarly jovial voice.

Standing in the centre of the room, his still smoking weapon pointing straight at Boswell's chest, was Robert E. Lee Sawyer, *né* Tarantyev.

But it was not Sawyer who had spoken.

Unbelievably, terrifyingly, standing by his side smiling widely in enthusiastic welcome, was Wardle.

15

Can I view thee panting, lying
On thy stomach without sighing;
Can I unmoved see thee dying . . .

MRS. LEO HUNTER

'Sit you down. Have a brandy. You too, Miss Allen. I'm touched that my resurrection causes such a shock. Of delight, I'm sure!'

Wardle bustled around them with every appearance of genuine concern while Sawyer looked on with sardonic amusement. The stout man was dressed in a modern sports jacket and trousers which looked strangely anachronistic on him.

'Nice of you to come back just at this moment,' drawled Sawyer. 'It makes walking out of here to our transport just that bit safer.

'What's going on, Jack?' asked Boswell quietly. 'Are you a double?'

'Hell, no!' Wardle sounded indignant. 'I've done a good straightforward job of work for years. With precious little thanks from things like *that*!'

He nodded with contempt at Swinburne.

'All right. What's all this about then?'

'Talking time's over,' interrupted Sawyer. 'Now it's walking time. We've got a schedule.'

'All right. All right. Get things organised then,' snapped Wardle.

Sawyer looked at him coolly for a moment, then went and spoke to the yellow-haired man who left the room.

'Who was it in the pond?' persisted Boswell. 'Colley?'

Wardle nodded gloomily.

'I'm afraid so. It was accidental; well, almost. He bumped into me in the barn, told me what was happening, that you'd sent him to get to the village. Well, I couldn't let that happen. There was a scuffle; I had to kill him. Afterwards I swopped coats with him. Mine was a bit distinctive and I didn't want anyone taking particular notice if they caught a glimpse of me around the place. And I didn't want anyone finding Colley's body either, so I lugged it round to the pond and slid it into the hole the Kraut had made.'

'We thought it was you,' said Boswell.

'Yes. I'm sorry.'

The yellow-haired man reappeared with a cardboard box. It was full of pairs of handcuffs. He started down the line of delegates, dragging their hands off their heads and manacling them behind their backs.

'Why did you have to disappear anyway?' asked Arabella suddenly.

'Well, it was this lot, really.' He nodded towards Thomas Traherne. 'As far as they were concerned, this was a nice quiet operation, just keeping an eye on what was happening here. We couldn't manage everything on our own and even with me in charge of security arrangements, it would have been bloody difficult to get a heavy mob in here, willing to do the work.'

His face lit up in a smile.

'Hey, ironic that! It was easier to get spies in here than ordinary criminals!'

The yellow-haired man had finished manacling the delegates and was now shackling their ankles with short lengths of chain, just enough to permit short steps.

'You leaked the news that the conference was on, of course,' said Boswell.

'Come off it, Boz!' protested Wardle. 'News of something like this is bound to get out. Hell, I could have sold tickets! No, I just made sure that Tarantyev here was kept especially well informed, so he managed to get himself in charge of the Soviet operation. But naturally these boys weren't very happy at the thought of blowing themselves. They had a nice little cover. The best! So we had to create a situation where it was necessary. First we stirred things up. I was missing, believed dead. You were running around like a blue-arsed flea. Everyone was after Tarantyev. Next thing, he's captured. Now, he'd laid it down the line, very big, what they were to do if he was captured. They didn't like it, but they did it. Well disciplined this lot.'

He nodded approvingly at Traherne.

'Came as quite a shock to them when they realised we weren't doing it all for Mother Russia.'

'You haven't told us yet what you are doing it for, Jack.'

'Haven't I?' His eyes were round with surprise that the question needed to be asked.

'Why, money of course! My days in the service are just about over, Boz. I haven't got a nice little alternative set-up like you. Literary scholar, grouse and port, touching up the students. No, it was the country cottage with roses up the wall for me. And I hate the bloody countryside! Friendly visits from old colleagues now and then—checking up to make sure I wasn't writing my memoirs and that no one was getting to me. No, I'd earned more than that.'

'So you sold out.'

'No! It's not like that. That would have been easy. And safe. I could have been having a nice steady income for years if I'd been willing to sell out. Any of us could, you know that, Boz. I'm no traitor. All we're going to do is auction three or four of this lot off! They're the top security men in their countries. What they know's worth a bob or two!'

So that was it. A multiple political kidnapping of a kind where the value of the kidnapped could be as great to another country as his own. It wouldn't be threats of their man's death that would make a country pay; it would be threats of his living somewhere else.

153

He glanced surreptitiously at the old clock against the wall where the blunderbuss hung. For Godsake! What were they playing at in HQ? Even Wardle couldn't have fixed it so that radio and telephone silence could be ignored for over twelve hours. Help must be imminent. There was no hope of Jimmy having got through yet, but surely someone somewhere would have acted by now?

'You realise they'll probably all end up behind the Curtain, Jack?' he muttered in a low voice. Wardle's defence of his patriotic loyalty looked like a weak link in the man's criminal reasoning. He doubted if he could cause a break, but even a delay might be useful.

'Nonsense!' laughed Wardle. 'They're too valuable to their home countries for them to let themselves be outbid. In any case, we're not going to be greedy. Half a million apiece will bring them back home.'

'If you squeezed what they know out of them, you could probably sell it piecemeal and make a lot more.'

'That's not the game,' retorted Wardle, angrily. 'Returned in good condition, that's the bargain. No one gets hurt, not even the taxpayers. This lot can be bought out of petty cash.'

'That might be your idea, Jack. But is it his?' He nodded at Tarantyev. 'You've both killed already. What's a bit of torture besides?'

'No!' protested Wardle.

'Don't get riled,' intervened Sawyer, who had been listening with broad amusement. 'The guy's just playing for time. He figures the cavalry's on its way.'

Wardle's face relaxed into a broad grin.

'Yes, yes! Of course! Boz, you're thinking all kinds of bells will be ringing in town! A general flap because there's nothing coming through from Dingley Dell! Don't worry your head about it. Every hour on the hour, they've heard us loud and clear. The Martlet's van is very efficiently kitted out with radio equipment. You didn't think I'd let a little thing like that escape me?'

No. He should have realised. It made good simple sense. And with Wardle himself on this end, who was going to worry about anything, especially on Christmas Day?

His posture must have shown his absolute despondency for Wardle clapped his hand comfortingly on his shoulder.

'Not to worry, Boz. None of it's your fault. We've been lucky, very lucky,' he said consolingly. 'Had to change our timing completely. It was all meant to happen last night, but the snow knackered things. We had to get the 'copter here and you can't fly those things in a blizzard. So everything had to be re-scheduled, and the longer you're at it, the more chance there is things'll go wrong, eh? Still, all's well that ends well.'

The door burst open and Wardle swung round quickly, revealing as his chatter had already done, how nervous he was. Momentarily, Boswell contemplated going for him, but the sight of Sawyer watching him coldly changed his mind.

Mrs. Hislop burst into the room, followed by another stranger dressed the same as the yellow-haired man. He too carried a gun and Boswell assumed he was the other arrival on the helicopter.

Mrs. Hislop was pale with anger. She strode boldly up to Sawyer.

'What's she doing here?' he asked his man.

'I've come to give you a warning,' she snapped. 'Both Herr Himmelstor and the boy Swinburne are very seriously ill. Unless I get them to hospital very soon, I can't be answerable for their survival.'

Sawyer continued to ignore her.

'The German bitch,' he snarled at the man. 'Where's she? You haven't left her?'

The man looked uncomfortable.

'She wouldn't come. And this one wouldn't stay. So I thought it best . . .'

'No matter,' said Sawyer. 'We're ready for off.'

'Aren't you listening to what I say?' screamed Mrs. Hislop. 'Don't you care what . . . ?'

Sawyer caught her a full-blooded back-handed blow on the mouth which sent her reeling back across the room, to end up on one knee by the wall. Sawyer went on as if the incident had never occurred.

'Now there's just one problem and that's that we can't take them all . . . There's a shortage of room unfortunately. So we're restricted to three. Mr. Swinburne and Mr. Leclerc are our first choices, you'll be flattered to hear. And our German friend too. But if he's as sick as this gabby dame says, then we'd better take one of the others. Any preference, Wardle, old son?'

'No,' said Wardle, looking unhappily at Mrs. Hislop. 'Anyone will do.'

'OK. Signor Brucciani, perhaps you'll join the trip. Harry, just see to these lucky people who are still wandering around free, will you?'

The yellow-haired man went over to Mrs. Hislop who must have seemed potentially the most violent person there and began to tie her hands.

'Where are the others?' asked Arabella. Boswell had almost forgotten her presence, so quiet had she been. Now he looked across at her and tried to smile comfortingly. She didn't look as if she needed it.

'Locked safely away,' said Sawyer amiably. 'Women and menfolk separately for decency's sake. Also each group's been told that any disturbance from either will result in indiscriminate shooting into the other. Always give people a good altruistic motive for not sticking their necks out! OK, you guys. Quick march!'

He was addressing the three delegates they were taking with them. Swinburne essayed a pace forward and nearly tripped as the chain between his ankles tautened.

'Take care there,' laughed Sawyer. 'We don't want to damage the merchandise before the sale.'

Leclerc, an expression of well-bred fatigue on his aristocratic face, spoke for the first time.

'If your interest in us is purely economic,' he said in his perfect English, 'why not cut down on your overheads and start the sale now? I do not doubt my government's willingness to pay handsomely for my return. A few minutes with your radio transmitter and I am certain I could give you a guarantee of the figure you seem to have in mind. It would save me considerable discomfort.'

He looked with distaste at the chain which shackled him.

Sawyer smiled but shook his head.

156

'A nice thought, Jules baby. But I don't know if I'd trust any guarantee from a Froggie. Besides, for a good sale you need lots of bidders. Now there's no one here competent to bid from my own country, is there? And who knows, perhaps even the Americans might be interested in buying themselves a slice of you. Very quietly, of course. You are an ally, after all.'

'Perhaps I can speak for the Americans,' said a new voice from the doorway.

Everything stopped. Every head turned. Standing just inside the room, wearing a dressing gown and looking very grey and tired, was old Bloodworth. In his hands was a long barrelled pistol which he held like a shotgun. The butt was very curious. Wooden, bound in red leather. It took Boswell a second to recognise it as the handle of the old man's stick.

'Uncle Sam!' said Arabella, anxiously.

Bloodworth smiled fondly at her.

'A fitting name, eh? Now please, nobody move. I appreciate I can't cover everyone, Mr. Sawyer, so I intend killing you if any trouble starts.'

For a moment Boswell thought he was going to get away with it. The two helicopter men looked questioningly at Sawyer. Wardle stood non-plussed by Boswell's side. Sawyer himself, his gun held slackly before him, seemed to be weighing up the odds.

Then Bloodworth coughed gently, his face went even greyer, he staggered slightly so that he leaned up against the door jamb, and his hand left the pistol barrel and went to his chest.

It was like a signal for action on a film set.

Sawyer's gun came smoothly up. Traherne standing handcuffed and shackled against the wall, hopped agilely forward and shoulder charged his former ally. They went sprawling to the ground together. Boswell hesitated a fraction of a second between going for Wardle and going for the yellow-haired man. It was a fraction too long, and Wardle caught him a back-arm blow across the bridge of the nose and sent him hurtling, half blinded with pain and tears, down the room towards the fireplace.

Bloodworth pulled himself together sufficiently to snap two

shots at the other helicopter man. The first crashed through the chest of the grandfather clock and set it chiming. The second caught the helicopter man in the throat and he slumped back with grotesque casualness into a huge armchair.

Arabella meanwhile had flung herself on Wardle and carried him to the floor bringing the tall Christmas tree down on top of them. Sawyer rolled clear of Traherne, rose to his feet and, his face contorted with anger, began to pump bullets into the man's helpless body. Even the yellow-haired man was transfixed with horror at the sight.

Boswell staggered to his feet, pulling himself up by the mantelpiece. Facing him on the wall was the old blunderbuss with the notice beneath warning all and sundry that it was loaded. Carefully he lifted it from its retaining brackets and turned back to the fray.

Wardle had beaten off Arabella who lay on the floor with a badly bloodied nose. Now the fat man was on his feet again, pine needles in his hair and a gun in his hand. Arabella grappled with his knees and, furiously, he kicked her off.

'Arabella!' cried Bloodworth, who looked in very bad shape. He had slid down the doorway and was now sitting on the floor. But he did not seem to have been hit and the pistol was still in his hand. He flung a shot at Wardle and missed by a yard. The bullet whistled by Boswell's head and smashed into the wall behind him.

Bloodworth would certainly have died now as Sawyer turned his attention from the dreadfully mutilated body of Traherene and brought his gun to bear on the old man. But in his fury he had emptied the magazine. Angrily he chucked the gun at Bloodworth catching him in the chest then bent down and took the wooden-butted pistol from the old, nerveless fingers. It looked for a moment as if he was going to use it on the helpless figure before him.

'Hold it!' yelled Boswell, advancing with the blunderbuss.

Sawyer turned and began to grin. Wardle shook his head warningly at Boswell. The yellow-haired man stepped into his path and raised his gun.

'Don't be stupid, Boz,' said Wardle in alarm.

He had cause to be alarmed. It had been an odd whim of

his own that had caused the blunderbuss to be renovated and rehung, loaded, on the wall. It made a fine jest to fire it out of the window in the presence of disbelieving guests. But it wasn't funny now.

Boswell pressed the trigger.

The noise was tremendous and accompanied by a huge cloud of smoke which parted to reveal what was left of the yellow-haired man's face registering complete disbelief before he sank lifeless to the ground.

Wardle had got the corona of the blunderbuss's fiery discharge in his right shoulder, and shieked out in pain.

Other fragments flew in the opposite direction where Leclerc, the only one of the chained delegates who had not sought what cover he could by dropping to the floor, received a few shreds of hot metal in his thigh but, after a single grimace, treated them with the same high disdain he had poured on the whole of the recent violent activity.

Sawyer reacted to all this with a typical wild-eyed laugh, brought up the pistol and fired.

The effect was dramatic. Arabella from her vantage point on the floor, saw Boswell stagger back a pace, surprise on his face. The now useless blunderbuss dropped from his hands, which he then clutched gently to his chest as though nursing a very tiny kitten. His knees sagged, he fell forward on them as though in prayer, and slowly toppled sideways. His legs twitched once and then he was quite still.

'Boz!' she cried in anguish. 'Boz!'

'You OK, Wardle?' demanded Sawyer.

'Yes. Well enough,' answered the stout man, looking round in what seemed like honest puzzlement at the carnage which surrounded him. 'I'm peppered in the shoulder, but not badly.'

'Let's go then. Say, with these two gone,' Sawyer said, indicating the helicopter men, 'We've room for two more passengers. Let's have ourselves some guilders, eh? Dutchy, you're coming for the ride. And what about . . . ?'

He didn't finish.

'Sawyer!' gasped Wardle. 'Look!'

He pointed out of the window. Everyone standing turned to look.

Halfway up the drive, belching snow into the air in a great continuous fountain, was a snow-plough. Behind it, just visible, appeared a Land-Rover. It looked very full.

'Come on. Move!' snarled Sawyer at Swinburne, ramming the pistol barrel into the small of his back.

'Go to hell,' gasped the Englishman.

'There's no time!' yelled Wardle. 'We've got to get out.'

So saying, he made for the door. Sawyer looked around the room, his lip curled back wolfishly. Then admitting the impossibility of getting the chained men out to the helicopter in time, he hurried out after Wardle.

Arabella immediately rose and went over to Boswell. Gently she poked him with her foot. He groaned and opened his eyes.

'All right, Humphrey Bogart. You can get up now.'

He sat up rubbing his eyes then winced as the movement brought a stab of pain from the graze which Tarantyev's bullet had left along his right rib-cage.

'I wasn't going to wait till he got the feel of the gun,' he explained. 'Did it look that obvious?'

'Dreadful,' she answered. 'Completely and utterly ham.'

But Boswell wasn't listening. He had risen and moved over to the window.

Sawyer was clambering into the helicopter behind Wardle. The snow-plough was still a good hundred yards away. The cavalry were not after all going to be in time. But a quick alert to the Air Force might still catch the fugitives before they could literally go to earth.

The radio in the barn. He could use it to summon extra help. His gaze turned automatically towards the snow-covered building.

There was someone there, standing almost out of sight. He couldn't make out who it was. One of the rescue party? Then why didn't he act?

The helicopter engine burst into life. The great rotors began to spin, gathering speed and strength. The snow-plough was very near but not near enough. The figure behind the barn stepped clearly into view.

It was Frau Himmelstor. She stood, stolid and inscrutable, watching the helicopter. Once more the snow on the ground was violently disturbed by the gale from the threshing blades. It rose into whirlwinds, swirling madly, settled again, then was lashed to life once more.

The helicopter began to rise. And Boswell saw it.

Out of the whiteness of the snow which had hidden it something ran in a dull silver line from the 'copter's undercarriage to the barn. He knew immediately what it was, how it had got there.

It was the long chain by which the tractor dragged tree-trunks down from the hillside. Only this time it wasn't the tractor that was doing the dragging.

The helicopter hovered a few feet above the ground as if Sawyer at the controls felt some impediment. But the snow-plough was very close now and men were jumping from the Land-Rover and scrambling through the snow towards the house. They were armed and one at least looked familiar to Boswell. But they were going to be too late.

The engine accelerated wildly, and the helicopter leapt mightily into the air, the two figures in it clearly visible through the translucent dome. Beneath it the chain ran out quickly till it was an arrow-straight line and the weight of the tree-trunk was suddenly added to the 'copter's load. It jerked visibly in the air and for a second it seemed that it might come crashing down. But Sawyer's superb reactions were able to regain control and he held the machine steady while he peered out to see what had happened.

The men from the snow-plough were firing up at him and Boswell now seized one of the discarded Sterlings, jumped through the window and ran through the snow, firing as he went.

Sawyer clearly decided that there was no time to rid himself of this impediment. The only answer was to take it with him!

The sound of the engine changed, the tree-trunk reared itself in the air like a caber at the Highland Games and finally swung

161

clear of the ground, causing those beneath to dive for cover as the great shillelagh came swinging at them.

If Sawyer had been able to afford a straight ascent all might have been well. But Boswell sent another hail of bullets up at the 'copter and the rear of the perspex dome frosted and starred in a most satisfactory fashion. This it was that probably stimulated Sawyer to move away as rapidly as possible. Still steadily gaining height, the helicopter headed off over the copse in which Boswell and Arabella had sought refuge a few hours earlier.

The machine itself was well clear of the trees, but the trailing trunk was not. There was a crackling of branches as it brushed the tops of the first trees. Sawyer must have been warned instantly by this of the danger. But for once his split-second reactions were not fast enough.

The trees were much taller in the middle of the grove. The trunk hit them, hard, then wedged fast.

For a second the helicopter seemed to hold absolutely still, a Christmas bauble gleaming in the pale sunlight. Then the image changed, and, like a bright new chestnut whirled destructively on the end of a young boy's string, the shining machine curved majestically through the air and crashed out of sight in the snowy meadow on the far side of the copse.

A moment later a great gout of flame leapt fearsomely above the tree-tops and Boswell, running with all his strength, knew there was nothing to be done. But he kept on running till the heat of the fire brought him to a halt.

He stood in silence then, and the melting snow ran in dirty rivulets around his feet.

'That was a hell of a thing, Mr. Boswell,' said a voice, beside him.

It was Jimmy, the tramp. With the instinctive expediency of his kind, he was warming himself at the raging fire.

'I met them, Mr. Boswell. They was on their way.' Jimmy recognised the necessity of honesty when he saw it. 'But I gave them your message. Do I still get my dinners?'

Frau Himmelstor was standing a little further round the ring of flames, gazing impassively into the holocaust. She moved a few steps closer, as if she were going to immolate herself on a funeral pile. She stopped, leaned forward with lips pursed and spat ferociously into the fire.

Such hatred. Boswell turned away wearily. All he could think was that twice in two days he had had to mourn the death of a friend. Once was once too much. Perhaps he was not the man for this business. He could see Arabella still standing at the parlour window.

'Yes. You'll still get your dinners, Jimmy,' said Boswell.

16

Although I have long been anxious to tell you, in plain terms, what my opinion of you is, I should have let even this opportunity pass . . . but for the unwarrantable tone you have assumed.

MR. SAMUEL PICKWICK

'I don't think she'd have cared if half the Crowned Heads of Europe had been in the thing,' said Boswell. 'She'd come downstairs, heard Sawyer refuse to do anything about getting poor sick Udo to hospital, and that was that. Out she went and hooked up the helicopter.'

'I'm glad she wasn't in the desert with Rommel,' laughed Halloway, the dapper little one-time tank-corps major who had been in charge of what he called 'the relief column'. 'How is poor sick Udo, by the way?'

'Still alive. If he survives the drive, he'll be all right.'

Himmelstor, Bloodworth and young Swinburne had been rushed straight off to hospital along the road opened by the snow-plough. Mrs. Swinburne, Frau Himmelstor and Arabella had accompanied them. Swinburne himself had felt it necessary to remain to try to salvage something out of the disrupted conference. There had been no time yet for a *tête-*

à-tête with him, but he had given Boswell a few what he interpreted as scape-goat-herding looks as he poured his oil on the troubled delegates.

The bodies had all been cleared away and the minor wounds of people like Boswell and Leclerc had been dressed by Mrs. Hislop, who had volunteered to stay behind for this purpose, showing no signs of resenting Arabella's usurpation of her position with regard to Bloodworth.

There was still a great deal of explanation needed there, thought Boswell.

But something like normality had returned to Dingley Dell. In fact, the genuine guests, once the emotional climax of their release and reunion was over, had rapidly assimilated the day's events as an incredible bonus of excitement on this unusual Christmas Day. They were at present in the dining room exchanging only slightly hysterical reminiscences and enjoying a cold collation organised by the long-suffering kitchen staff. A strange difference noticeable between these guests and those more closely involved with the dramatic events of the day was their clothing. The guests still wore their Dickensian outfits as to the manner born, whereas the delegates without exception had changed into modern dress.

'So really all we did by getting here,' said Halloway, 'was to save old Swinburne and a couple of foreigners? I wonder, was it worth the rush?'

'What made you come anyway?' asked Boswell. He hadn't yet had time to put this question. There had been much to do.

'Simple really. We were checking up on Bennett, the guy who didn't turn up, and Sawyer as well of course, when Wardle came on to say not to bother, Sawyer was all right. You'd searched his gear and found conclusive evidence. A bit vague, but coming from Wardle good enough. Until some masochists who spend Christmas morning splashing in the briny down at Southend turned up, rather sick, at the local cop-shop with bits of body. Identification was almost instantaneous. A very neat man, Mr. Bennett. Name tabs on everything, even expensive, hand-made shoes. So the police turn up at his flat at lunchtime. Our boy on watch there makes himself known. And bingo! we have a very odd situation. So we don't ask, we just set out!'

'Be welcome to Dingley Dell,' murmured Boswell. Poor Wardle. See how the world its veterans rewards . . .'

'Wardle was being watched, you know,' said Halloway suddenly. 'It's always a dangerous time in a man's career. But you had to give it to him. He was good. We never got a sniff, certainly not of any connection with Tarantyev. It would have been better for him if we had. Tarantyev was mad. His masters will be glad to see him go. He got too many kicks out of this kind of action. Even if the helicopter could have got in last night, he'd have found some excuse to start shooting. And Wardle wouldn't have lived to spend his share of the loot.'

'He didn't,' said Boswell.

Swinburne appeared and beckoned imperiously to Boswell.

'The conference is reconvening in ten minutes. I want coffee and sandwiches available right through. Also let me know the minute my wife gets back from the hospital.'

'Sir!' said Boswell in an NCO's bark.

Swinburne eyed him narrowly.

'It might be necessary for you to say a few words to the delegates,' he said slowly. 'So hold yourself in readiness. Remember, they're experts. They have an expert interest in this business. Later, there's your own part in all this to be discussed.'

His tone was completely neutral. Leaving himself the option of giving me a medal or sticking my head on London Bridge, thought Boswell. He wants to come out smelling clean as possible.

He made arrangements for the refreshments, then made his way to the filing room. There were one or two things he wanted to look at. None that he hadn't seen before, but they might make a new kind of sense now.

Arabella returned alone from the hospital about twenty minutes later. She was pale and drawn. Boswell knew instinctively what had happened.

'I'm sorry,' he said.

'He just went. No pain.'

166

'Did he say anything?'

'Only, *now it's yours for real. Enjoy it.*'

She looked at Boswell as though trying to assess if this made sense. He nodded.

'What he left to you, he meant? He was your uncle, the one who "died" in South Africa?'

She nodded in her turn.

'That's right.'

'A CIA man?'

'That's right too. Your files weren't that good, were they? He was always the adventurous one of the family. Merchant seaman for a while; then he joined the US Marines. That's where he was recruited. He was never terribly important, just a good competent operative.'

'When did you find out?'

'In South Africa,' she said. 'We used to quarrel terribly about South African politics. It wore him down in the end, I think, keeping up the pretence for me. So he told me.'

'And recruited you?'

She laughed.

'I suppose so. I doubt if I was any use. When I worked for Cerberus, I sometimes heard things. It brought in some pin money, but I felt so furtive about it that it wasn't worth it. Then Uncle Sam died.'

'You believed that?'

'Oh yes,' she nodded emphatically. 'I was desolated. He was all I really had. When I saw him here, I could have killed him! All that grief for nothing. But when I talked to him, it was all right. Things had started getting hot for him. If he just got out, everything he had would have been confiscated. So he decided to die! That way he disappeared legitimately— drowned at sea—and I inherited legally.'

'And Mrs. Hislop? What about her?'

'Well, he came back here, meaning to contact me. Then he had his first heart attack. He was very ill. I was making my way slowly north through Africa at the time. His colleagues fixed for him to be treated by Mrs. Hislop. Her husband had also been in the business and while she was never active her-self, she knew enough about things to be discreet. He recovered. They got on very well together, he had to live somewhere, it was a good cover and she was agreeable, so he became her old Uncle Bloodworth, who, as I'm sure you checked, really existed.'

'A universal uncle, eh?' smiled Boswell.

'He was mine. I loved him,' she said simply.

'And how did you both happen to turn up here?'

'He fixed it, I suppose. He was put on this job because everyone expected it to be so quiet. No one regarded your conference as being very important, not at this stage anyway. So it was a nice way of keeping Sam on the payroll and at the same time letting somebody else spend Christmas at home with his family. But Sam wanted Christmas with his family too. He can be—could be—very persuasive! It was suggested to me, gently but persuasively, that if I had nothing better to do at Christmas, I might enjoy myself here. And if I kept my eyes and ears open, I might find something nice in my Christmas stocking. But it wasn't the money, it was just feeling bored that made me agree.'

'Well, well. So after all, you're one of us,' breathed Boswell.

'Does it make any difference?' she asked.

'Only that I can now seduce you without qualms! But one thing first.'

'Only one?' she said provocatively.

He ignored her.

'What was he doing trying to get out of the house last night?'

'He wanted a look at the pop group's van.'

'What the hell for?'

'Curiosity. Natural suspicion. He felt something was wrong. The CIA had checked your guest-list too, of course.'

'Had they now!'

'But of course. Very thoroughly. When I told him about Sawyer—that's when you saw me in his room—he immediately came to the conclusion that he couldn't be working alone. As you yourself began to suspect. And the only people in the house he hadn't run a personal check on were the musicians. So he thought their van might be worth a look.'

'He was dead right,' said Boswell gloomily. 'I wish to hell he'd shared his theories.'

'Well, he wasn't exactly an invited guest himself, was he!' retorted Arabella. 'You'd have probably put him under lock and key. In fact that's exactly what you were aiming to do when you chased him and he had his attack.'

'I'm sorry,' said Boswell gently.

'No. It wasn't your fault. He shouldn't have been doing it. He was like Traherne, just there for a quiet bit of keyhole-peeping really. Sawyer was the one who stirred things up.' She spoke bitterly.

They were interrupted by the Fat Boy, who was gnawing a leg of goose.

'They want you,' he said between chews. 'In the conference room. Ten minutes?'

'Right,' said Boswell, glad to change the mood of the conversation. 'Hell, I nearly forgot. The others. How are they?'

Himmelstor was doing well, though his face would probably need plastic surgery. And Stephen Swinburne had recovered consciousness. Both the other women had opted to spend the night at the hospital in case there was any change.

'I had a long talk with Mrs. Swinburne,' said Arabella. 'Girl-to-girl stuff. And I said hello to the boy too. Interested?'

'Give!' said Boswell. Five minutes later, well pleased with what he'd heard, he left the room. On the landing a figure stepped out of the shadows and took his arm. It was Suzie Leclerc.

'The boy,' she said. 'How is he?'

Boswell eyed her narrowly.

'Not good,' he said finally. 'May I talk with you?'

He was twenty minutes late at the conference.

The atmosphere in the conference room was strangely intimate. Like old soldiers who have unexpectedly found themselves under fire again, the delegates seemed to have set about recapturing the spirit of 'old times' and Boswell shuddered to think of the stories of undercover 'derring-do' which must have been exchanged.

Briefly he told Swinburne about his son and his wife.

'Good. Good,' he said with great relief. 'Gentlemen, gentlemen, your attention please. Herr Himmelstor is well, you

169

will be pleased to hear. And my son has recovered consciousness.'

There was a murmur of pleasure at the news.

'Mr. Boswell,' said Leclerc casually. 'Do you know yet how Stephen came to be injured?'

'Yes, I think so. He had the misfortune to run into Wardle, who could not afford to be seen after arranging his own mysterious disappearance.'

'So it was Wardle who struck him down, not Tarantyev?'

'That is so.'

The Frenchman nodded and relaxed in his chair. Swinburne began to speak.

'Gentlemen, Mr. Boswell is much more closely connected with the field-work surrounding this conference than I. I have already apologised for the events of today. But as you all know the aim of good security is not to achieve the impossible. Any attempt to do so would be to invite complete and abject failure. No, we must be pragmatic. For a conference like this to be organised without any leaks at all would be miraculous. Miracles are *not* our business.'

There was a ripple of amusement. Encouraged, he pressed on.

'And where *prevention* is impossible, *cure* becomes all important. That's what we have seen today, gentlemen. Cure. Though the walls were breached, the defences held and the gap has been closed. If when the turn of *your* country arrives to host this conference, you can offer me that assurance, I shall be satisfied.'

He sat down. The delegates nodded approvingly. Boswell groaned inwardly.

'Mr. Boswell.' It was Brucciani. 'You have acted well and bravely. And I agree with what Mr. Swinburne says. But perhaps you could tell us, briefly, what you feel in practical terms could have been done to strengthen these walls which were so easily breached. I ask, not in a critical spirit, but in order to learn.'

Latin irony of a high order, thought Boswell, rising to his feet. He felt Swinburne's cold, warning gaze on him.

'Gentlemen,' he began. 'We were at a disadvantage from

170

the start insomuch as the whole context of the conference was conceived by the man who betrayed us, Wardle. In fact those elements which he claimed would give maximum cover—that is, the Christmas holiday in a hotel—were just those elements he needed to make his own plans work. So lesson one is, do your own planning.'

Swinburne looked displeased, but nodded agreement.

'Lesson two follows from lesson one. If you can't trust your own lieutenants, then you're a fool to trust anyone. Even the people coming to the conference.'

There was an excited murmuring. Swinburne was glaring furiously at Boswell but he pressed on.

'Don't look offended, gentlemen. Everyone is permitted a few peccadillos. If, Signor Brucciani, you wish to bring your mistress instead of your wife, that is your affair, I suppose. Though we would have preferred it if you had brought a mistress who wasn't also bestowing favours on a gentleman from the Polish Embassy.'

Now there was real uproar, with English abandoned for the moment. Eventually Leclerc's precise voice pierced the din.

'My dear Swinburne, even with Wardle dead, your underlings leave much room for improvement.'

'That's enough, Boswell,' rapped Swinburne. 'I'll talk with you later.'

'I'm not quite finished, sir,' said Boswell politely. 'Monsieur Leclerc, you must not feel attacked. There is no doubt whatsoever that Madame Leclerc is your legally wedded wife. What is odd, however, is the way you encouraged her to use her charms to invite the boy Stephen Swinburne to attempt the theft of confidential material pertaining to this conference.'

Now all the clamour of Babel filled the air, so much so that the worried Fat Boy, on duty outside, opened the door and peered in to see the cause of the disturbance. Swinburne waved him out angrily.

'Leclerc,' he said loudly, 'I apologise. Believe me, this man will pay. Boswell, leave now or I'll have you arrested.'

'Wait,' said Leclerc. 'I have been accused. It interests me. I should like to hear the basis of this fantasy.'

171

'Certainly,' said Boswell. 'You never wanted this conference to succeed. Whether the opposition is private or official, I do not know. Nor whether it's absolute or merely relative. Perhaps a conference in Paris would be a more fitting place for success, eh? No matter. It's one of life's little ironies that interference on such a large scale as we have seen was being planned. You weren't to know that as you pushed your own small spanners into the works.'

'Scintillating metaphors,' breathed Leclerc.

'Young Swinburne was the main one. That's what he was doing the night he was attacked. Encouraged by your wife, he was helping himself to documents from his father's room. What would have been the next step I do not know. Contact with the newspapers? Or perhaps you just planned to have him caught. Whatever the case, it was interesting that much of the stuff he found in his parent's room shouldn't have been there. These for instance. Conference minutes.'

He pulled a sheaf of papers from his inside pocket and chucked them on the table—Swinburne looked at them in amazement.

'Fortunately Miss Allen, into whose room the boy was carried by Madame Leclerc after she found him unconscious in the corridor, had the wit to conceal these and show them only to me.'

'I don't understand,' said Swinburne. 'I never took such papers from the conference room. It would have been a gross breach of security!'

'No. But Leclerc did. It would have helped to discredit you personally as well as the whole conference.'

'Interesting,' drawled Leclerc. 'But I deny it completely. Does the boy say this? A fevered imagination stimulated by the blow to his head.'

'Not just the boy. Your wife also,' said Boswell grimly. 'You may care to go to her. To get the truth, I had to tell her the boy was on the point of death. And if you'll excuse me, gentlemen, I shall go also. I think I've had enough of answering your questions.'

He turned and headed for the door. Swinburne overtook him in the ante-room.

'Why the hell didn't you tell me all this personally, you fool? We might have salvaged something. By God, how we could have used this information!'

'Go to hell, Swinburne,' said Boswell wearily. 'Think yourself lucky I didn't tell them all in there that your son's a member of a student group so far left it makes Traherne seem like Disraeli, that you knew this, and that your wife had given you a pretty good picture of what was going on early last evening. She told Miss Allen everything. How Stephen had told her he was a member of InterPax and had come to Dingley Dell to try to wreck the conference. He wanted his mother to leave you, did she tell you that? Luckily for you, she's a woman of strong loyalties. Like me. So I won't tell the others. They probably know about Stephen, anyway. Leclerc certainly did. That's how he knew the boy could be worked upon. Not that he needed much work, though. The slap-and-tickle was just a bonus. The only reason he had for spending Christmas with his ever-loving parents was so that he could balls-up the whole operation. And you know what? I'm beginning to think he was right!'

The door made a most satisfactory slamming noise behind him.

17

'You shouldn't have said that,' said Arabella.

'Perhaps not. I was angry.'

'I take it you're resigning?'

Boswell began to laugh.

'That's an understatement! I wonder if I can reclaim my superannuation?'

'Not to worry. I've got plenty.'

He sat up in bed and looked to where he could see her opening a bottle of Scotch by his dressing table. Her naked body gleamed gently in the moonlight pouring in through the window.

It was still only nine o'clock on Christmas Night. Below from the ballroom they could hear sounds of merriment. The festivities were continuing as though nothing at all out of the ordinary had taken place during the day. It would need a pretty big carpet for all the recent events to be swept under, but it was a pretty big broom that was doing the sweeping. And with the telephone still not officially working, the hotel guests could be kept cut off from contact with the outside world, at least until Boxing Day.

For Boswell, however, the festivities below had no attraction. He was much happier where he was.

'What do you mean?' he said. 'I'm not a pauper. I've got my Fellowship. And my books.'

'Fellowship and a book at bedtime. Is that the best you can offer?'

'Hurry up with that drink and we'll talk further.'

'Just a sec. No ice.'

'Never mind.'

'Wait.'

She went to the window, opened it and looked out. The sky was now completely clear and the moon was at its full.

'There's a draught! What are you doing?'

'Getting some snow. Scotch and snow. How's that for kinky? The new Christmas drink!'

'Christmas. What a hell of a way to spend Christmas. Not what Dickens had in mind.'

'This?' she said, mock-offended.

'No. That,' he answered. 'Close the window and come to bed.'

'Wait,' she said again. 'What's that?'

'What?'

She was staring out of the window. After a moment he climbed out of bed and went to join her, shivering exaggeratedly.

Coming down the drive towards the front of the house was a small flotilla of lights, bobbing and weaving.

'What is it?' asked Arabella once more.

'I don't know. The Russian Army, perhaps, come to blow us off the face of the earth.'

'Don't talk like that. Wait a minute! I see what it is,' she said excitedly. 'Lanterns. Boz, it's children with lanterns.'

'Oh no,' he said, leaning out. 'You're right. It's the carol-singers. They should have come last night, but the blizzard kept them away. No one can have told the vicar.'

'Told him what?'

'What indeed?' said Boswell.

'Still, if there's a vicar out there, I'd better cover up.'

She went to the wardrobe and slipped on Boswell's dressing gown, then returned to the window. The children had reached the front of the house now and grouped themselves in a semicircle. Someone below must have spotted them too for suddenly the record player which was substituting for T.T. and T.T.H.M. faded away and the noise of voices died down.

The vicar stood in front of the children and raised his hands.

The children's voices, a little cold and uncertain at first but rapidly picking up in strength and enthusiasm, launched into *God Rest Ye Merry Gentlemen*.

They listened in silence for a few minutes. Boswell thought of Wardle. *Be you welcome to Dingley Dell*. Of Thomas Traherne and his young men. Especially the bass guitarist who had watched with such delight the hare leaping through the snow.

'Merry Christmas,' said Arabella, leaning back against him and breaking into his melancholia.

Suddenly it seemed a possibility after all.

'Merry Christmas,' he answered.